Tribal Law

Miscreants & Magick

Shannon Curtis

Inspired by readers, for readers

Tribal Law: Miscreants & Magick, Book 1

Copyright © Shannon Curtis 2015

First published March 2015

ISBN: 978-0-9942422-0-4 (print edition)
        978-0-9942422-1-1 (ebook, Smashwords edition)
        978-0-9942422-2-8 (ebook, Kindle edition)

Edited by Jennifer Brassel
Cover design by EBook Indie Covers
Typeset by Debbie Phillips, DP Plus

Published by Australian Romance Readers Association Inc.
www.ireadromance.com.au

Dear Reader,

One of the most common questions ever asked of an author is 'where do you get your ideas?' For *Tribal Law*, I can say—I got it from you.

In June 2014, it was pointed out by book blogger and reviewer, Book Thingo, that there were no local reader events for the month of July. When the authors at TWC Press heard this, we approached the Australian Romance Readers Association with a concept. What if there was an event where readers could tell authors what *they* wanted to read in a story? And what if the authors took all that information and wrote *that* story? And what if the authors *gave* that story back to the readers?

The Australian Romance Readers Association thought it was a novel idea—and the ARRA Project was born. On 4 July 2014, seven people got together and hashed out details. From character names, descriptions, quirks, occupations etc., to genre, heat level and cover preferences, they made suggestions, and the team from TWC Press made notes. Then we collated this information, and plotted out a story. We now present *Tribal Law*, the book plotted by readers, for readers.

The work involved in creating this story is donated by TWC Press to ARRA—and to all readers. All proceeds made from the sale of this book go directly to the Australian Romance Readers Association to help readers. We hope you enjoy reading this novel as much as we enjoyed discussing it, plotting it, writing it and sharing it with you.

Sincerely,
Shannon Curtis

P.S. As this novel is published by the Australian Romance Readers Association, and written by an Australian author, the spelling and language used is Australian English. We hope you enjoy!

Dedication

For all lovers of romance fiction—thank you for reading our stories.
You demand excellence, and by challenging us to deliver it, we authors grow in craft—and in heart.

Chapter One

The trick with working with teeth was to make sure your patient was relaxed, preferably unconscious. Ryder Galen's patient was neither.

"Let go of my hand," he said succinctly, gazing down into the alpha's silver eyes.

"You're hurting me," Jared Gray growled as he tightened his grip on Ryder's wrist.

Ryder fought the temptation to roll his eyes. Jared was Alpha Prime to the Alpine Pack, and would take insult—and then take his business elsewhere. His practice was just starting to pay for itself, and listing Jared Gray as a client would net him more valued clients. He couldn't afford for the werewolf to take his business elsewhere.

"Your lateral incisor is loose, and it's going to have to come out. Of course it damn well hurts. If you'd let me sedate you ..." Ryder let his voice trail off in suggestion.

Jared shook his head. "No. I don't do drugs. I don't like being out for the count, and I don't like the hangover afterwards."

Ryder turned back to his tray of implements. Jared didn't trust him. He could understand. Most shifters—as well as most vampires—didn't like feeling vulnerable or exposed. Some baulked at using an anaesthetic, which meant there was a lot of hand-holding, a lot of soothing ... a lot of damn tears. He hadn't realised his job would be part miscreant dentist, part den mother. Fine. He had to work on building those trust relationships. Hard to do when even he didn't trust anyone as far as he could spit. He sighed. "Okay, but try to control your beast. If you keep grabbing me every time you feel a twinge, we'll never get this done."

Jared nodded, then gradually loosened his grip. "Fine. Do it."

Ryder went back to work, gently moving the loose tooth. He must have pulled on a nerve, because Jared's growl was cut off mid-morph and suddenly Ryder had a pain-enraged wolf beast on his hands.

He jumped back as the silvery wolf swiped at him with his claws, and dodged behind the upright lamp. The wolf lunged toward him. Ryder dived behind the reclined chair, hearing the leather rip under the scrabbling of the lycan's claws.

He made a mental note to add that to the alpha's bill.

The wolf leapt off the back of the chair and landed on braced feet before turning like wind in a vortex to face Ryder.

Ryder was ready, swinging his arm in a punch aimed at the wolf's jaw. The wolf howled as he fell to the side. Ryder launched himself at the lycan, lowering his head to avoid the snapping jaws of the beast. He grappled with the creature, wrestling it to the ground. The alpha was in great shape, conditioned over a lifetime to hunt and fight. Ryder hissed as a claw sliced across his bicep, the hot burn fuelling his anger as the wolf reared over him.

Ryder curled his hand into a fist and summoned his power. He slammed his fist into the snout of the beast, channelling his lightforce into the contact. His white light blasted the wolf back into the wall behind him. The wolf sagged to the ground unconscious, leaving a concave dent of cracked and crumbling plaster in his surgery wall.

The alpha could pay for that, too.

Ryder sat up and checked his arm. It was a deep cut. He was going to need stitches. He'd have to add it to the other scars criss-crossing his body. Getting bitten and scratched was an occupational hazard for a miscreant dentist. He rose to his feet and stared down at the wolf he'd knocked out cold.

"Told you to let me sedate you," he muttered.

He washed up, his movements quick and efficient as he tied a rough bandage around his arm to stem the flow of blood. Working quickly, he hauled the limp body back onto the chair and used straps attached to the headrest to hold the lycan's mouth open, then proceeded to remove the left maxillary lateral incisor. Using suction, he cleaned the hole, then started to mix the binding agent for the replacement tooth. He should have a dental assistant for these tasks, but that type of job had a high mortality rate. A lot of dental nurses just didn't have the skills to fight off a raging miscreant. As a light warrior, Ryder had a special skill set for addressing miscreant's dental needs, not least of which was being able to hold his own against the fierce creatures.

Most of his patients required removable dentures, but Jared could afford the privilege of a permanent prosthodontic. Ryder was using a new acrylic material, one infused with morphing minerals. He painted the base of the prosthetic tooth with the goop he'd just mixed, and inserted it into the gap in the gum. He channelled his light, focusing it on the tooth. Like tendrils of rampant ivy, his light twisted and rolled over the tooth, over the base, and into the nerve endings, securing the new tooth to the wolf's jaw. Working with miscreant teeth was difficult, especially with changelings. You had to factor in the shapeshifting, the morphing of the jaw structure, and the difference in teeth from man to wolf—or bear or leopard or any number of animals. This tooth would look slightly bigger in his human form, but only just, and would be in scale for his wolf form when he shifted—which would be when he'd most need it.

He held the tooth in place, patiently waiting for it to bond to the nerve and gum. Jared flinched, just a little, and Ryder frowned. The alpha still remained unconscious, but his breathing was becoming shallower, faster. The wolf flinched again, his back arching. A low-pitched whine came from his throat, before foam started to build in his mouth. Ryder winced. Not good. He lifted an eyelid to check his patient's status and recoiled. The eye was blood red. No iris. No pupil. Just a sack of crimson within the eye socket.

Hell.

He stood up. The wolf started to quiver, then thrash on the chair, a garbled growl coming out of his throat as the straps broke under the force of the movement, the foam bubbling forth from his slack jaw.

What the hell was going on?

The wolf started convulsing. Ryder laid his hand on the beast's forehead, sending warmth into the mind, searching for the pain in an effort to soothe. The muscles in his jaw flexed. That couldn't be right. He tried again, extending his senses as he did so.

He could only sense darkness—no, not a darkness, more like a … nothingness.

The wolf jerked his head to the side. Ryder cringed at the sound of vertebrae snapping before the wolf subsided, sliding down into the chair as though boneless.

Ryder checked his patient, feeling for a pulse, for a breath … for a heartbeat. Nothing.

He closed his eyes and swore.

An alpha prime had just died in his surgery.

He was dead meat.

* * *

Vassiliki Verity checked her watch. Good grief. She still had twenty minutes left on her pro bono stint. The night was becoming damn near interminable. Still, it was just twenty minutes. She glanced around the courtroom.

A werewolf paced in the 'cage'—a fortified cell designed for the super-strong lycans—as his case was read out to the judge. He'd killed someone, but fortunately for the justice system, he'd killed another of his kind.

She shook her head. Maintaining your beast's form was the highest insult to the judge, and she could see the judge's annoyance. The lycan's representative smoothed down his tie as he finished his plea.

"So you see, Your Honour, as this is a murder-by-kind charge, we'd like the defendant to be released to the Woodland Pack and for the matter to be handled under the tribal jurisdiction."

The judge sat back in her chair, steepling her fingers. She stared at the wolf in the cage for a moment, arching an eyebrow as its low growl rumbled across the courtroom. Vassi winced. Yeah, it wasn't a good idea to mouth off at the presiding judge.

The judge smiled sweetly at the defender. "You are right. This is a matter for tribal law, but," she held up finger as the defender's shoulders sagged in relief. "The victim was of the River Pack, and the incident occurred in River Pack territory—"

"That's disputed territory," the defender argued.

"Not by the courts, it isn't," the judge said smartly. "Defendant will be transferred to River Pack Remand for tribal judgment." She hit the gavel on her block. "Next."

The wolf bared his teeth and this time his growl was loud, long and menacing.

The judge responded by baring her teeth right back, her incisors lengthening as she hissed at the lycan, her eyes glowing. "Settle," she rasped, her voice deep and booming. The wolf reluctantly subsided as the bailiff secured a collar around the wolf's neck and dragged him back down the caged tunnel to general holding.

Vassi leaned her head against the wall and closed her eyes. This would be the last case before her pro bono shift ended. She tried to make herself comfortable. She'd head home via Mad E Pizzeria, pick up a meatlovers pizza, type O with extra anchovies, hold the garlic, and crack open that bottle of shiraz that remained in her wine rack while she read over the Marchetta files. She'd be back at the office tomorrow and would have to compete with her associate, Lara Dyson, for the case. Lara was a real bitch, and not just because she was a lycan. Ever since Vassi had joined the firm Lara had made it her mission to poach each case that came anywhere near her. At this rate she'd struggle to make budget.

Vassi forced herself to take a calm breath. Everything would be fine, she'd work on the Marchetta case, win it, and the boss would take her off probation.

It was a few minutes before the partition at the end of the tunnel re-opened and Vassi heard the jingle of chains as the next defendant entered the room. An uproar started at the rear of the public area. Vassi sat up to look over her shoulder. Lycans, all in human form, were gathered near the doors, growling and showing their teeth.

It took the judge a few minutes to call for order. The group eventually settled, but it was obvious they were a whisker away from exploding again. Alpine Pack, from the looks of their pale complexions and fair colouring. She turned in curiosity to see what had caused the ruckus, but the prosecutor blocked her vision of the man inside the cage.

The court clerk read out the docket. Vassi tuned out as she tried to remember which charge Vivianne Marchetta was facing now, subsiding in her seat to once again shut her eyes. Another disappearance, perhaps.

"You don't have representation?"

Vassi cracked one eyelid open warily at the gently phrased question from the judge.

A deep rumble was the defendant's response, she couldn't quite hear the actual words.

"Verity, you're up," the judge called out to her.

Both of Vassi's eyes startled open and she looked at the bench.

The judge beckoned her to the front of the room. "You've got a case."

Vassi picked up her briefcase and rose, making her way along the bench and apologising to folks as she hurried by them. The lycans in the crowd glared at her before reluctantly allowing her to pass. She made it to the central aisle and hurried through the swing gate at the front of the room.

"Judge …" her mind went blank as she made eye contact with the judge, then a word whispered to her mind. "Judge Flack, I ask for the court's patience while I assess my client's case."

The judge frowned. "It's Judge Roberts," she corrected.

Vassi waved a careless hand. "I know, but I think Flack suits you much better. May I see the report?" she held out her hand to the prosecutor. Oh, good. Taylor Henley. One of the few names she actually got right. Ever since she'd broken up with his douchebag of a friend, he'd taken great care to avoid her in the courtroom. This should be fun. The shifter prosecutor handed her the file.

"We ask that the matter be transferred to Alpine Pack jurisdiction," Henley stated calmly.

"Objection, Your Honour," Vassi said automatically, then scanned the pages quickly to find the basis for her objection. Ah, there. "The crime did not occur in Alpine territory, so does not fall under Alpine jurisdiction."

"Due to the nature of the victim, the law does make allowance for jurisdiction transfer under these circumstances," Henley argued.

Circumstances? She blinked when she read the details of the crime. Good grief. He'd killed an alpha prime.

Her eyes widened and she looked up, finally seeing her client for the first time.

Pale blue eyes met hers. His dark brows were pulled low, yet she couldn't quite read his expression. His face bore the dark shadow of a beard, except for a line that bracketed his mouth. The visible scar didn't really detract from his looks— although it did add to the lethal air about him that was only enhanced by the cuffs and penal uniform. He also sported a bruise or two. She wondered whether he'd gotten them killing an alpha prime, or whether any of the werewolves in detention had attacked him. He had jet black hair, the length a little long for her personal taste, and looking tousled, as though he'd wrestled with a bear—or an alpha prime. He was big, too. Well over six feet tall, the bright orange jumpsuit he wore pulling tight across broad shoulders, yet drooping and baggy around his waist and hips. His hands clasped the bars of his prison, the chain dangling down to the manacles around his ankles.

"Uh ..." He'd killed a friggin' prime.

"Do you have any objections to the transfer of jurisdiction?" the judge prodded her.

"Uh ..." If she said nothing, his case would be out of her hands, she'd be free to return to work as per normal, take on the latest Marchetta case, pretty much cement her position at Campbell, Singh & Partners—and hopefully Lara Dyson could choke on a fur ball.

She glanced toward the back of the room. Saliva was dripping from some of the lycans' teeth, and they all shifted, as though ready to charge. He wouldn't stand a chance.

She pursed her lips. Ah, crap.

"Yes, ma'am, we do."

"On what grounds?"

Hell. What grounds? She looked down at the folder in her hands, thinking fast. "Ah, while a pack can request jurisdiction transfer if a member of the prime family is the victim, this request can only be made by the alpha prime. In this case, the victim was the alpha prime so Alpine Pack currently has no recognised alpha prime, therefore no request can be officially made."

There. She sighed in relief.

As one, several lycans at the rear of the room growled. Oh, great. Now she'd angered the lycan population. Honestly, she must have a knack for pissing off wolves.

"Order!" The judge rapped her gavel until the growls subsided to a general low rumble. She then surveyed Vassi for a moment, a considering look in her eyes. She nodded. "Fair enough." She looked at Henley. "Request denied. How does the defendant plead?" She asked blithely over Henley's protests.

"Just a moment, Your Honour," Vassi said, holding up her finger and crossing to the dock. She peered closely at the man behind the bars. His gaze drilled into hers like a silver laser, powerful in its intensity. "How do you plead?" she asked quietly, meeting his eyes and forcing herself not to look away.

"Not guilty," he muttered, his voice a low rumble.

Sensation washed over her, warm and pleasant, but with a tinge of coolness. Vassi frowned slightly, then turned to the bar. "Not guilty, Your Honour."

"And bail?" the judge asked as she jotted a note down in her ledger.

Henley took a deep breath, clearing the frown off his forehead. "We ask that the defendant be remanded in custody."

"Objection, Your Honour. We request the defendant be released on his ..." Oh, crap. With the lycans on the hunt for his blood, releasing the man on his own recognisance would be the equivalent of a death sentence.

"Into your custody? It's unusual, but I'll grant it. Bail is set at two hundred thousand dollars for release into Ms. Verity's custody," the judge stated, hitting her gavel on the block.

Vassi blinked. Er, what? She glanced at Henley, who looked equally stunned. Did she just—?

"This is most unprecedented, Your Honour," Henley protested.

Vassi nodded. Hell, yeah, it was. She didn't want to be responsible for the man. Since when did a lawyer take her clients home with her?

"Relax, Sir Prosecutor. Trial is set for—" the judge glanced at the court clerk, who checked the schedule.

"We have a space in the schedule for Monday, Your Honour. A case finished early this week."

The judge nodded. "Great. Monday it is. Next."

"But wait—" Vassi called out and took a step toward the bench. Things were happening way too fast here, and she couldn't quite catch up. "I haven't had a chance to confer with my client, nor to prepare a suitable defence."

The judge smiled. "I'm sure Sir Prosecutor can arrange for all relevant material to be dispatched to you immediately. You have the weekend." The judge stopped smiling. "Next."

Vassi snapped her folder shut and leaned down to pick up her briefcase. What the hell just happened? She started to walk toward the swing gate into the public gallery, but stopped when Henley blocked her path. The man was big, bigger than her defendant—but then, most bear shifters were like human mountains.

"Accept the transfer request," he told her bluntly.

She snorted. "He won't last the road trip. No, we'll hear the case here."

"You don't want to do this, Vassiliki. It's going to get bad. Dump the case."

She blinked. So they'd gone from Vassi to Vassiliki. She knew he was creating distance by using her formal moniker, and not the nickname most of her friends used. Damn Kelvin. "Sorry?" It took her a moment to register the rest of his words. Did she just hear Sir Prosecutor correctly?

"Take a look around. All lycans will be out for his blood—he killed a prime. A non-pack member killing an alpha prime outside of tribal warfare is an insult not only to that alpha's pack, but to all shifter tribes. He's a walking dead man."

She glanced toward the rear of the public gallery. The men back there were angry. Hands fisted, teeth clenched—they were ready to launch. "Everyone deserves a trial." She was relieved with the calm tone she'd managed, despite the anxiety of seeing a wall of lycan rage ready to pounce on her.

"This guy handed himself in, Vassiliki. The evidence is overwhelming."

She cocked her head and looked at him. "Why are you so concerned? I thought you hated me."

Henley sighed. "I don't hate you, Vassiliki. You hurt my friend, I'm just being loyal."

"Hey, he hurt me first." Taylor had introduced her to Kelvin, the bear that should really be an ass. When they'd broken up Taylor had naturally sided with his jerk of a mate—and she could only imagine the stories her pathetic ex had made up. Since then, Taylor had avoided working any of her client's cases where possible—until now.

"I just don't want to see a fellow officer of the court in danger. Anyone who helps your client will be fair game."

Vassi's eyes narrowed and she bared her fangs, just a little. "Tell anyone who is thinking of coming after me that I bite."

"What if they bite first? You vamps don't stand a chance against a werewolf bite."

Vassi patted him on the arm as a smile lifted her lips. "Why Taylor, anyone would think you cared."

"I don't *hate* you," he said with exasperation. No, he was just blinded by loyalty to his douchebag of a friend.

"Ms. Verity!"

Vassi turned to face the judge, who indicated the man being led back down toward the holding cells. "Perhaps you'd like to accompany your client."

Vassi hesitated. Nobody ever wanted to go back to the urine-drenched, sweat-stenched holding cells. She glanced back toward the rear of the public gallery. But then, she didn't want to try and push her way through that mob.

"Certainly, Judge Flack."

"Roberts."

"Whatever."

Chapter Two

"I still can't believe the judge did that."

Vassi grimaced as she held the phone between her ear and shoulder, and fumbled for her day-planner.

"Me, neither," she muttered to Seraphina, the personal assistant she shared with two other junior lawyers at the firm. "I'm going to need to reschedule some appointments next week so I can do this case."

"Okay, I've got your diary up on screen now. Hmm, everything else you can move, but you have a meeting with Ms. Marchetta on Wednesday."

"Don't reschedule that, for God's sake. I need the Marchetta case."

"Yeah, well, you're going to have to touch base with your client. RB is definitely on the scent."

RB was Seraphina's nickname for Lara Dyson. The assistant reasoned that as the daughter of a werewolf alpha prime, Dyson really was a royal bitch. Vassi didn't disagree.

"She's got her own clients, damn it. Singh gave me this file and I want to keep it."

"Tell that to RB," Seraphina suggested sarcastically.

She'd tried to, and RB—er, Lara—always smiled and nodded, yet Vassi could sense the lies. It had become a game of chess as each associate tried to outmanoeuvre the other. Sometimes Vassi won. Sometimes ... not.

"Oh, wow, I just pulled up the booking photo online of your hottie," Seraphina breathed.

"Client, not hottie."

"Well, I'd be happy to play handcuffs with him."

Vassi sighed. Seraphina was a cambion; half-human, half-succubus. To say she had an active sex drive was an understatement.

"Well, I just need to get him off, and then I'm all Marchetta's."

"Oh, hon, I'd love to get him off."

Vassi wheezed a laugh. "Seraphina, don't you have any standards? The guy is a criminal."

"One: yes, I do have standards—he has to be great in the sack. Two: he's not a criminal yet, and if you get him 'off', he won't be."

Her thoughts went back to the man in the cage, his hands holding the bars, his pale blue stare boring a hole through her as he rumbled his plea. She shook her head. There was no way she could entertain any thoughts of an entanglement with her too-hot client.

"Can you please just reschedule my appointments? I won't be in the office on Monday."

"Uh, if you need any help with taking notes, research, humping the bejeebus out of our client, you just let me know, okay? The prosecutor has just sent through the files, I'll forward them on to your remote account."

One of the things that had drawn her to Campbell, Singh & Partners was their use of technology—and their inclusive employment program. As one of the rare firms that hired different breeds of miscreants to represent any number of tribes, working there provided the ability to hone a very diverse skills base. Employment with Campbell, Singh & Partners gave any associate the experience across all major tribal jurisdictions, ergo, any associate became a very attractive hire and could virtually name their price in their career journey. The firm was always adapting to the latest innovations and modifying them for the different races. She'd be able to access all the files through an online, secure interface—she could work from anywhere. If they'd just take her off probation. She held the dubious honour of being the longest-serving probie.

"Thanks. See you next week." She disconnected the call and pulled out her laptop to get to work.

* * *

Vassi glanced at her watch once more. Seriously, how long did it take to check out of holding? Her client apparently had just enough funds to pay his bail, but the wheels of bureaucracy turned slowly. It had been over two hours. At this rate the pizzeria would be closed by the time she got there.

"Galen!"

She stood up and collected her briefcase as she crossed to the main desk. The cop shoved a clipboard at her and indicated she sign there, there, and there.

"Where are you taking him?" the officer asked casually as he drew the clipboard back from her.

She frowned. "Pardon?" She dropped her gaze to his name badge. Officer Perkins. Funny. He looked more like a Thomas.

"The alpha killer. Where are you taking him?"

Hell, she hadn't thought that far ahead. If she took him to his home, she was sure there'd be a pack ready and waiting for him. If she took him to hers, she was just inviting trouble home with her. She wasn't about to admit she had no clue. "What's it to you?"

Officer Perkins quickly scanned the immediate area. When he was satisfied there was nobody within earshot, he leaned forward, baring his fangs. "I heard some of those dogs back there. They want his scent. You watch yourself, Verity."

She nodded slowly, then jumped at the sharp clang of a lock sliding back in the silver gates. She turned as her client walked out to greet her.

Hoo-wee. He now wore jeans and a belt with buckle that looked like some sort of military coat of arms. His long-sleeved t-shirt moulded to his massive biceps and pectoral muscles before skimming his flat stomach. She swallowed. He was big. Built. Beautiful. She blamed Seraphina and her lusty comments for her momentary lapse in assessing him as a potential bedmate, not a client. It took her a moment to notice the rip in his sleeve and the stained bandage beneath it. Blood. For a moment, she enjoyed the awakening of her senses, the faint scent of rust beneath his natural fragrance. But only for a moment. She quashed the awakening, despite the temptation to push up against him, just for a little taste.

He walked up to her, his shoulders rolling gracefully with each stride, and stuck his hand out to her. Her mouth dried as she watched his hips swing. Good God, the man could move.

"Ryder Galen," he said. She tried to keep his name clear, but her customary mental fog obscured it. His voice was smooth, deep, and just the right timbre to relax her tense shoulders. She frowned. She wondered if the alpha had been relaxed, lulled into a false sense of security, before he died. She tried not to stare at the scar on his face. It looked to be an old injury, yet the man didn't have a record of violence.

"You look more like a Max."

He did. All he'd need was a leather jacket and a Harley-Davidson to straddle, and everyone would call him Max. She refused to think of what else he would look good straddling.

Her client blinked. "What?"

She nodded. Yeah. Max. "I'm going to call you Max."

"My name is Ryder," he said, frowning.

She clasped his hand. "Vassiliki Verity," she responded, ignoring his remark, along with the warmth spreading up her arm from his touch. Damn, he was potent. A hot gaze and an even hotter touch. No, she wasn't going to turn all giggly and mushy for this man, despite Seraphina's suggestions. She'd sensed a chill from him in the courtroom—she didn't trust him, not at all. She pulled her hand from his warm clasp and clutched the handle of her briefcase.

"You're a miscreant dentist," she said, a little surprised. She'd read his file—she'd had nothing else to do for the past two hours in the waiting room. Miscreant healers were a rare breed, skilled and trained to care for all the 'miscreatures'. His eyes narrowed as he slowly nodded. Goosebumps rose on her arms. A murdering dentist. Surely that had to be even a miscreant's worst nightmare?

"I understand you turned yourself in," she said. That was unusual. It was possibly why Judge Flack treated him so favourably. "Why?"

"I figured it would buy me some time. If the lycans discovered the body before the authorities, I wouldn't get a trial. This way, at least I get a chance to prove my innocence."

A chill brushed her shoulders and she averted her gaze. He wasn't being completely honest with her. Well, that was no surprise. Each of her clients always maintained their innocence, no matter how guilty they were. Still, he had a point. If the lycans had discovered the alpha prime's body, her client would have been slaughtered on the spot. Now, though, he was protected by the law—until his trial, anyway.

She'd seen the lycans in the courtroom, though. If they could get to him beforehand, they would.

"Do you have a car nearby?"

He nodded. "I parked just down the block."

They started to walk toward the door. "You couldn't know how long it would take to get back out on the street—or *if* you'd get back out on the street. Weren't you worried your car could be stolen?" Especially in this neighbourhood. Everyone seemed to ignore the nearby police presence and did whatever the hell they liked. Another reason she hated these pro bono stints. The calibre of client she gained usually left a lot to be desired. She flicked her gaze at her new client. Okay, so a few people might desire this one. He was her client, and if her ability was anything to go by, he'd had a hand in the murder of an alpha prime. Vassi had learned the hard way to pay attention to her gift; she wasn't about to start ignoring it now. She trotted down the steps, trying to keep up with his long stride. Her gaze darted around. The sky was lightening, with plenty of shadows for vengeful lycans to hide in.

"I wasn't worried," he said quietly, his eyes straight ahead as he strode down the street.

Vassi clutched the handle of her briefcase even tighter. The man made no effort to check his surroundings. She might have fangs, and she might know how to use them, but she always exercised caution when walking down dark streets. She was a half-creature of the night—she knew what could be out there.

He halted in front of a dark red Honda Civic and tugged the keys out of his pocket.

Her eyes widened. "You've got to be kidding."

His eyebrow rose, and she knew he was just expressing surprise, perhaps curiosity, but the quirk of his eyebrow suggested a sexy wickedness. No, damn it, he was a client. A lying, murdering dentist, for crying out loud.

"You drive a hatchback?"

He nodded.

This she had to see. How the hell did he fit inside?

He stilled, then his head whipped around. She heard nothing, but the hairs on the back of her neck stood up, and a faint breeze stirred her hair right before she was knocked to the ground.

Chapter Three

Ryder whirled, dodging the snapping jaws that tried to tear out his throat. He grabbed a fistful of fur and threw the attacking wolf over the hood of his car, using the wolf's momentum to do so.

He turned to help Vassiliki up, but the woman threw her head back, her brown hair tumbling over her shoulders, her fangs glistening in the light cast by a street lamp. Her warm brown eyes turned to molten gold and then red as she rose to her feet. In one sleek, graceful move, talons slid out from the tips of her fingers, the lethal blades dark and slim.

Cute fangs.

A blurry shadow caught his attention. He turned. Another lycan, this one all tawny and sleek, barrelled toward him, teeth bared. The first wolf pounced on his back and he stumbled, twisting around as he fell. He gritted his teeth as the wolf dug his claws into his shoulder.

Then the wolf flinched, howling as it sprang away. Vassiliki stood behind, a talon dripping with blood. The wolf turned on her, head low, snarling.

Ryder arched his back and sprang to his feet, facing off against the golden lycan. He realised it was female, yet her size was greater than he'd expect. She halted in front of him, turning one way, then the other, gently herding him back toward his car.

He knew what she was doing. Backing him into a corner. Any other time he'd launch his own attack—but not now, not with her. He'd never seen her before, but he suspected he knew who she was.

"Samantha?" He held up his hands as though to soothe Jared's mate. "I swear, it's not what you think."

Her lips curled as she snarled. He could see her anger—but he could also see her pain.

"I didn't kill Jared, and I'm going to prove it."

She sat back on her haunches for a moment, sitting tall and beautiful as she assessed him. "I'm all about making my patients feel better—not killing them. Something happened—I don't understand what, but I aim to find out."

He was getting through to her. He could see the keen intelligence in her eyes—right before she pounced on him.

* * *

He woke to a dull throbbing in his head and a muttering in his ears. He opened his eyes, wincing at the flashing lights. He blinked. Everything was upside down. It took him a moment to realise he was in his car, his seat fully reclined, his feet hanging outside the front passenger window.

"… and you couldn't drive a normal car, no sirree. Damn it. You had to drive something a leprechaun could fit in."

He twisted around, wincing at a twinge in his neck, the burn in his shoulder. His lawyer was driving his car. She was safe. He closed his eyes briefly in relief, battling the resurgence of the memory of another woman, the life draining out of her. No. Wrong time, wrong woman. His lawyer was safe. He looked at her. She now bore little resemblance to the woman he'd first seen in the courtroom, all prim and proper and coolly beautiful with her red slimline dress and black jacket. She'd lost her jacket, her bodice and sleeve were ripped, and her hair hung about her shoulders in tousled brown waves. Her skin was pale, almost translucent, making her brown eyes even more striking in contrast. Now she seemed vibrant, simmering with an energy that was magnetic. He wondered if she consciously hid her passionate instincts, her vitality, behind her austere professionalism, or if she was even aware she did it.

He remembered the instant when she'd let her instincts surface. His lawyer was a bit of a vamp—but only a bit. He'd seen her fangs. Not quite as prominent as a full-blood vampire, they were more delicate in size and shape, but no less lethal, considering she'd faced off against two werewolves. Oh, and the talons …?

"Oh, you're awake. About time," she snapped, glancing his way. Her eyes were nearly brown again, only a faint glow remaining to add fire to her glare. "Do you know how hard it is to get a six-foot-plus deadweight into a damn hatchback?"

"What happened?"

"We nearly died, damn it. Why didn't you hit her when you had the chance?"

He levered himself up in the seat, pulling his feet into the car. "Because I didn't have any reason to," he said as he fumbled with the seat release, wincing as the backrest jerked upright.

"No reason? She was about to rip your throat out."

"She's just angry because I killed her mate."

He turned at the choking noise, and she lifted her hand from the steering wheel for a moment, shaking her head. "Don't say any more, Max, for God's sake. Not yet."

"My name's Ryder." He turned to look out the window and frowned. "Where are we?" The car was heading down a highway and he could vaguely make out the shape of dark mountains against the pale grey sky. He didn't see anything familiar in the landscape, though.

"We passed Lake Selwyn about an hour ago. Should be coming up to Summercliff in a few minutes. We'll stay there for the day, then get back on the road in the evening."

"Why?"

"Well, considering the welcoming committee that was waiting for us at your car, I can't imagine the reception you'd get at your place. I'm guilty by association, so I don't think my place would be any better. This is part of the Nightwing territory, so we should be safe enough."

She had a point. Wolves would be reluctant to trespass into vampire territory. He took a deep breath. He'd known he was a marked target—hadn't realised it would affect his lawyer, though. Regret tightened in his gut at what he'd already put her through—and what was likely to come their way.

"I'm sorry."

"Should have thought of that before you killed an alpha prime."

"I didn't kill him," he retorted, then sighed. Damn. He knew he was contradicting himself, but he was confused as all hell. One of his patients had died under his care—there was no getting away from that. But he sure as hell hadn't committed murder. He didn't know what had caused Jared's death, but he hadn't wanted to kill the werewolf. "I didn't want him dead."

"You don't need to convince me, Max. My job is to defend you whether I believe you or not."

She met his glance briefly, her eyes narrowed and darkening to a deep black, as though she was trying to peer inside his skull. He ignored the sting he felt at her words. He'd heard a lot worse in the cells, and nobody had believed him there, either. Her gaze dropped to his shoulder, and the golden glow in her eyes flared briefly before she blinked and looked away. He looked down. His shirt was torn and bloodied. And he was sitting in the car with a vamp—yet felt no threat. Interesting. Belatedly he realised she was driving as the sun started to glimmer across the tops of the mountains. He frowned.

"Are you okay? Shouldn't we find someplace for you to take cover?" He'd seen what happened to vampires caught in the sun.

She shook her head. "I'll be fine." A sign appeared on the road ahead, pulling her attention, and she took the turnoff into Summercliff.

"You're a daywalker?" That was rare. Every moment he spent in this woman's company just made him more intrigued. What was she that she could withstand a touch of sunlight? He found himself wondering what other touches she could withstand ...

"Does this tin can have chains?" She hadn't answered his question.

He blinked, trying to shake off the mental images that were causing his blood to heat. "Hey, Blanche is a beauty, don't insult her. Chains are in the boot. Why?" She had to mention chains. Visions of her chained to a bed, her eyes glowing as he caressed her. What would she look like out of that prissy little outfit?

Vassiliki turned to him for a moment, her mouth agape, then she finally blinked. "You're a dentist, you drive a hatchback, and you named it Blanche. I don't think you could possibly be any more of a nerd."

His eyebrows rose, successfully distracted. Nobody had actually called him that before. At least, not to his face. "Why do we need the chains?" he repeated, this time his voice almost a growl.

"We're going to need them where we're going."

"Where are we going?"

"Alpine territory."

* * *

Vassi glanced around the motel room, wrinkling her nose. The once-cream carpet looked grey wherever it wasn't stained. The brown curtains reeked of cigarette smoke, and the bedspread on the one queen-sized bed in the room looked like a clown had thrown up all over it.

But when she had pooled her available cash with her client, this was about as much as they could afford. She'd had to use the corporate credit card, too, but hopefully the small amount wouldn't set off any alarm bells in the finance department just yet. While they were an equal opportunity employer, Campbell, Singh & Partners was predominantly staffed by werewolves. She crossed to the TV and turned it on, surfing the channels until she found a twenty-four-hour news station, and felt the usual sense of comfort as the low hum of conversation played like a soothing soundtrack in the background.

"I'll take the floor," he said from behind, and she turned to catch a fleeting expression of distaste cross his face as he gazed down at the filthy carpet.

"Thanks, Max." She sure as hell wasn't about to share a bed with an alpha killer, no matter how smoking hot he was.

She gestured to his shoulders. "We should get you cleaned up. That has to hurt." They'd stopped off at a pharmacy on the outskirts of town where she'd bought some supplies— along with 'I love Summercliff' t-shirts for both of them.

His shirt was torn, ripped in shreds across his shoulders, and the scent of his blood, sweet and seductive, with a hint of unfamiliar spice, called to her. For now, she could resist the temptation, but the sooner she got him patched up, the better for both of them. He frowned at her. She assumed he was noticing her attire. Her dress wasn't much better. Damn it, it was her favourite power outfit for work.

"Why do you do that?" he asked, his voice muffled by fabric as he pulled the shirt off over his head.

Thank God his face was hidden. Vassi gaped at every exposed inch of skin. His chest was sharply delineated by corded muscle, his stomach banded with a smooth, sleek six-pack. No eight. No—good lord, more? She raised her hand before she realised what she was doing, and had to snatch it back before she touched him. She pretended to casually play with her hair instead.

She'd dated a few werewolves—and maybe vampires, a jerk of a bear, changelings and an angel or two—in her time, and most of them sported chest hair. The man who stood in front of her was all smooth golden skin, apart from the alarming number of faint, silvery scars criss-crossing his body like the coloured veins in a block of carved marble. Quite simply, he was beautiful. She wasn't bothered by his imperfections—she had her own, after all, and perhaps it was his imperfections that made him damn near perfect.

"What?" Had he said something? Was she supposed to be talking? Damn, look at that chest. A pale slash marred one pectoral muscle. It must have hurt like the blazes at the time, but it had the light sheen of aged scar tissue. Her gaze followed the line. It stopped just short of a dusky nipple. She licked her lips as it pebbled in the cool air of the room, then bit her lip. Damn, she needed to get back in the dating scene as soon as she could shirk this nightshift. She was getting all hot and bothered over a client, for heaven's sake. A lying, murdering client. Maybe Seraphina could fix her up on a blind date.

He hissed as he peeled the cloth where it had stuck to cuts on his shoulders, then bunched the fabric up into his hands and tossed it at the bin in the corner. The bunch and flex of his muscles was mouth-watering.

"You called me Max. My name is Ryder."

What? Oh, right. They were supposed to be holding a conversation. She picked up the first aid kit from the bed and walked toward the ensuite. "You seem more like a Max to me."

"But I'm not. My name is Ryder."

The mental fog hazed over his words. She was hopeless with names. Her mind threw alternate, more fitting names at her, to the point it obscured the person's real name. A quirk of her gift, her mother had told her. But she didn't need to mention that to all and sundry. Let them think she was hopeless with names, or just plain rude. She put the toilet lid down and gestured for him to sit while she readied the first aid supplies. She had to distract herself. With his dark hair, pale blue eyes and lips made for kissing, he looked like wicked sin incarnate.

Then she turned and her gaze was drawn to that impressive chest—and his wounds. She had a weakness for blood, but her human compassion won out. She winced. "Oh, Max, that's got to hurt."

He shot her an exasperated look as she dampened the washcloth and gently cleansed his cuts. They were silent for a while as she gingerly wiped away the congealed blood and dirt. Surprisingly, they'd survived an encounter with two werewolves. That was rare, and she still wasn't quite sure why the tawny lycan had retreated once she'd knocked him unconscious against the car. She wet the washcloth, wrung it out, then cleaned his shoulders and chest. Once she got control over the blood temptation, it was quite easy.

Her hand glided over the smooth pectoral muscle, tracing the scar, and she watched as his skin pebbled with goosebumps under her cool ministrations. She wanted to lean down and lick his nipple. Vassi swallowed as heat warmed her cheeks. She looked up and met his gaze. He was watching her watch him. She drew the cloth back up to his neck, smoothing it over his shoulder, feeling his gaze on her like a hot flame.

"So, tell me about yourself," she said huskily as she wet the cloth again, wrung it, and went back to gliding the cloth over his skin. His gorgeous, golden skin. She really should get to work on those cuts. She ran the cloth from his shoulder down over his arm, skimming across a bulging bicep, then blinked. He had no cuts on this arm, she just wanted to stroke him. She tossed the cloth onto the counter and started digging into the first aid supplies.

"What do you want to know?" His voice seemed husky, too.

She shrugged. She just wanted him to talk to distract her from groping him. "Why did you become a dentist? No, wait," she said, holding up a cotton ball. "Why did you become a miscreant dentist?"

He frowned. "I hate that term, you know?"

"Dentist?" She nodded with a shudder. "I hate that, too."

"No, I mean miscreant. Miscreatures. There are so many of us ... vampires, werewolves, shapeshifters, changelings—perhaps we're not miscreatures at all."

She arched an eyebrow as she upended a bottle of antiseptic on a cotton ball. "What are you? You seem human."

"I am, mostly."

She pressed the cotton ball to one of his cuts. He didn't even flinch. "Mostly human? How does that work?"

"Well, you're not a full vamp, are you?" His hand rose and he lightly clasped her chin, gently pulling her lip down to expose her teeth. His touch spread a warmth through her chin and face, and she was tempted to lean into the contact.

"Half-blood," she admitted. He still held her, his gaze focused on her mouth. She swallowed as she stepped back. He appeared reluctant to let her go. "You know your teeth."

"Is that why you can walk in the sun?"

"Yes. It's uncomfortable, but not dangerous." She turned back to get more antiseptic.

"What else?" he asked, his gaze intent.

He'd neatly side-stepped the question. Fine. She could work with that. "I can walk in daylight, I can control my bloodlust better than most, and verbena and silver sting, but they're not lethal to me."

"But? Your humanity seems to offer some strengths, so I'm pretty sure it cuts both ways. How does your vampirism affect you?"

She shrugged. "I don't have the full strength and speed of a vampire, and I don't seem to be able to compel." At least, not without help. She was sharing, but she wasn't stupid. She didn't give away any of the weapons she depended upon for survival. She decided to turn the focus back on him.

"So, what made you choose dentistry?"

"Family business."

"You—you're family are dentists, too?" Oh, her nerd-finder was flashing lights and ringing bells. She dabbed at more of his cuts.

"My father and brother are dentists," he told her. "Actually, my brother is an adept, so he can work in all healing disciplines. I worked with them for years, but now have my own practice." She focused on her senses. There was warmth there, yet still accompanied by the soft breeze of deceit. He was mainly telling the truth, but there was more to it. Maybe not so much a lie, but an omission. He'd definitely lied to her in the car, though. She could sense it when he discussed the death of the alpha. She sighed. Her father may have been a vampire, but her mother was a truthseeker, so she'd inherited traits from both sides of the family, one of which was her own built-in B.S. meter. It was a great tool in the courtroom and corporate negotiation—not so much on the dating scene, though, and she'd learned not to ask "does my butt look big in this?"—it never ended well.

"Are they miscreant dentists, too?"

"Yeah."

"Why did you branch out on your own?" She'd had to visit a miscreant dentist once, when she was a teen and she'd been run over by a werewolf in full stride. A complete accident, but she'd needed a little work on her central incisors as a result. While in the surgery she'd seen a vampire go full bloodlust on a dentist. That didn't end so well—at least, not for the dentist. No wonder his body looked like a road map for the metropolis of Irondell. "It's a dangerous job. Wouldn't you want the security of a large practice with backup?" Preferably armed backup, with enough horse tranquilisers to knock out a den of wolves.

"I wanted to create my own destiny, work my own way, take on my own clients."

While there was a thread of truth here, the overwhelming wash of cool deceit was undeniable. Not quite a truth, not quite a lie. Her incisors lengthened as she cut a length of tape and covered his wounds with gauze. She was finished. She didn't have any more excuses to touch him. She reached out to smooth an imaginary crease in the tape. Okay, she really did have to stop petting him.

She gathered the supplies, tossing the rubbish into the trash and led the way back into the bedroom. A news bulletin was just starting.

"Why are we heading into Alpine territory?" he asked as he wandered into the room behind her. She had a spare t-shirt for him, but refrained from offering it. He seemed comfortable enough walking around bare-chested, and it was probably better for his injury if he limited movement, like dragging on a t-shirt.

Oh, look, her own B.S. meter was going off.

"I'm not sure if there are any lycans there, they all seem to be out hunting you. It could be the safest place for you." Or not. "I'm doing this pro bono for you. I don't have a truthseeking investigator on my payroll, so we're going to have to do our own research to offer another explanation at trial as to what happened." She didn't bother to disclose her own talents in that area.

Her client sat on the end of the bed and folded his arms. His biceps bulged with the movement. "What were you thinking?"

"Jared was an alpha prime," she said as she crossed to her handbag sitting on the bedside table. "There has to be some competition for that position. We'll see if we can come up with an alternate theory to what happened."

"Like what?"

She shrugged as she withdrew a vial of lipstick. "Like a reason one of Jared's pack might want him dead." She sat on the other side of the bed and scooted up to rest her back against the bedhead. "Did you kill Jared?" she asked carefully.

She relaxed, opening her awareness.

"No, I did not kill Jared."

Liar. That phrase had a significant chill to it, the fog in her mind clouded by a dark trail of deceit. She slid the lid off the lipstick and twisted the bottom. "What happened, Max?" she asked, curious to see what he'd come out with.

He shot her a quick glare at the use of the name, then shrugged. She marvelled he felt no pain at the movement. Years of working with miscreants had toughened him. "Nothing. I was working on him. And then he died."

Okay, so that was truth, but it still left a lot unsaid. "But you didn't kill him?"

"No." This time the chill was almost a burn to her senses.

She took the compact mirror out of her bag and quickly, casually, applied her lipstick. It was a vibrant scarlet, blood red. Her mother had a sense of humour. She carefully retracted the lipstick. It was an old family recipe that compelled folks to tell the truth. As a half-blood, she lacked the ability to compel, but her mother's side was well-versed in the art, with loads of little tricks to drag out the truth. Unfortunately there was only one way to get others to expose themselves to this particular dose. She glanced at her client who was staring at her lips, his handsome face almost disturbing in its intensity. Her heart pounded just a little faster. For once, she was going to enjoy this.

She dropped the compact and lipstick back in her bag, then rolled up onto her knees.

His eyes met hers as she advanced on her hands and knees, prowling across the bed like a kitty on the hunt. A line appeared on his forehead, as though he was surprised—or maybe confused—yet definitely interested. She paused in front of him. Suddenly the confusion was replaced with something more—an awareness, a hot desire that energised the very air between them. Her gaze dropped to his mouth. She could feel his breath against her lips, and her own breath hitched. They paused there for a moment, as though enjoying the closeness, the anticipation.

Oh, yeah, she was definitely going to enjoy this.

Chapter Four

Vassi leaned forward and pressed her lips to his. She infused the contact with her gift, anchoring her ability to the emotional essence of the man she kissed.

For a moment he didn't move, and she pulled back. His lips bore the sheen of her lipstick.

"Tell me what happened," she whispered.

His gaze flickered, glazed over. No creature could withstand the compulsion. "I killed him," he whispered back, and she knew a moment of intense, burning disappointment. Nothing but warmth washed over her. He was telling the truth. "He was in the chair. I painted his tooth, I applied it, and he reacted. I don't know why," he admitted huskily. Again, more warmth. His confusion was an honest reaction. Then he did something unexpected. He leaned forward to press his lips against hers.

She quivered, his lips like a brand on hers as he pressed harder, widening her mouth. His tongue slid inside, toyed with hers. Oh, God. Her breasts swelled, and heat curled inside her. She tore her lips from his. Damn it, this was supposed to be an interrogation, not a seduction. She swallowed.

"Why did you kill him?" she asked softly, then didn't try to dodge as he kissed her again, his tongue darting inside her mouth before he retreated, blinking.

"I didn't kill him," he said huskily, then shifted closer to her on the bed. Warmth washed over her in a wave, and she frowned in confusion. Two statements that contradicted each other, yet both registered complete honesty. She braced a hand against his chest—oh, God, his skin felt wonderful beneath her fingertips—and met his gaze.

"Tell me exactly what happened," she said, licking her lips. His gaze remained fastened on her mouth, and he nodded as he leaned in to her.

"Okay," he murmured. His hand delved into her hair as he kissed her again. This time he kissed her thoroughly, his tongue sweeping into her mouth as he held her head in position. Long and languorous, his kiss turned into something hotter, darker, as he explored, using her mouth as a carnal playground. He would pull back and start to talk, then lean in to kiss her again. Then repeat the process. For the first time, Vassi found it difficult to keep track of the conversation as he simultaneously relayed the events of Jared's death and drove her crazy with desire as he bore her back down on to the bed.

Eventually she pressed her hands against his chest, breathless. "Okay, I think I've got it," she said, gazing at his mouth. He blamed himself for Jared's death, but hadn't intentionally caused it.

"Are you sure?" he said, leaning down to drug her with more hot kisses. Okay, this was going way further than a truthseeking mission. She was all hot and trembling, and if she didn't stop soon, she'd be incapable of thought, let alone resistance.

His hand trailed down to her breast, and she shuddered as he palmed her flesh through her clothes. Sweet Jesus. Maybe just a little longer. She arched her back, pressing herself into his hand, then heard her name in the background. She broke off, panting, and turned to the TV. "Wait—what?"

A reporter stood on the steps of the courthouse, giving details of the death of Alpha Prime Jared Gray, the man accused of his murder, and the lawyer defending him. The man she'd named Max pulled back from her and turned to face the television.

"Ryder Galen, son of Arthur Armstrong, will return to court on Monday to face trial. Mr. Armstrong had this to say about his son's case, earlier this evening."

The scene cut to a well-dressed man who looked to be an older version of Ryder, handsome in his maturity, who paused briefly for the microphones and cameras on his way into his car.

"Of course we're upset by what's happened with Ryder. The accusation is horrifying, but he's still my son, and has my support. We'll help him in any way we can."

"Do you think he's guilty?"

Arthur Armstrong stared down the eye of the camera. "We're all capable of committing murder, but my son is a good man." Armstrong sent a forbidding glare at the reporter, then stepped inside the waiting limousine, shutting the door with finality on the reporters.

"And so we wait to learn more of the details regarding this alleged murder by the Deviant Dentist."

* * *

Ryder stared at the TV as the news team crossed back to the studio. He blinked. He felt like he was waking up from a deep sleep—and in a rather jolting way. His father's defence of him seemed almost sincere. Convincing, yes, yet Ryder still remembered why he'd left the family. Sometimes his father went too far in defence of his sons. That sense of bitter disappointment still burned like an ember in his gut.

"What the hell?" Vassiliki gasped as she slid from the bed, her mouth open as she switched her gaze from the screen to him. "You're Arthur Armstrong's son? You lied to me. You told me—you told the court—that your name was Galen," she accused, her hands on her hips. Her torn bodice gaped open, displaying a satisfying amount of cleavage and a scarlet and black lace bra. He wanted to tear that garment off her. He frowned. He was hard, so damned hard. How was it that he felt so damned aroused? It was embarrassing, particularly as they were just talking. He wondered what his lawyer would think if she knew the lustful thoughts running through his mind, that he wanted to reach out and finish—what? His mind was blank, despite the lust gripping his body. Yeah, embarrassing. His frown deepened at her words.

"I didn't lie. My name is Ryder Galen."

She gestured to the TV. "Are you going to tell me the reporter was wrong, that you're not part of the Armstrong family?"

"Not anymore."

She glared at him. "What do you mean, not anymore?"

"I told, you, I left the family."

She held up a finger. "No, you told me you left the family business. You just failed to mention that your family is part of the criminal elite." Damn it, she wore a look as though he'd betrayed her. He hadn't.

He rose up from the bed, frustrated on so many levels. He tried to live a separate life from the rest of his family, yet at every turn he was judged by a relationship he refused to acknowledge. He hadn't spoken with his father or brother in months—not since *that* night. He refused to be in the same room, let alone share the same name.

"You never asked who my family was—I never lied to you about them. The family business *is* dentistry. Everything else is rumours and innuendo." No charge was ever laid against them—at least, not one that would stick. His father and brother enjoyed a powerful position in Irondell's society, and you didn't reach that level without treading on people's toes—or graves. He'd walked away from all of that, but he wasn't going to betray his blood.

"Oh, is that the official PR spin?" She tilted her chin up, her eyes bright with anger.

"What does it matter who sired me? I walked away from him, my brother, and the business, months ago."

She gaped at him for a moment, as though struggling to understand the concept. She folded her arms. "Well, it looks like he'd welcome you back to the bosom of the family in a heartbeat."

A muscle flexed in his cheek. Some things came at a high cost, and returning to the cold embrace of his family was a price he simply wasn't willing to pay. He'd already lost too damn much to them. He was finally putting his life back together, finally finding some peace, some happiness. Until now, that is. He frowned. She was angry, but he had no idea why. This got more of a reaction from her than his murder charge.

She turned from him for a moment, then looked at him over her shoulder, her expression calm, remote. "Why don't you hire a lawyer? You can obviously afford one. Why settle for a public defender?" A line appeared on her forehead.

He sighed. "No, I can't. I really did walk away from everything. I haven't spoken to my father or brother in months. I changed my name, and I borrowed heavily to open my practice. I surrendered any claim to the Armstrong name and fortune when I took my mother's maiden name."

She gazed at him, searching his face for something, he didn't know what. Apparently satisfied he was telling the truth, she sighed as she faced him. Again, his gaze dipped to the tempting flash of silk and lace. "At least he defended you."

Ryder smiled grimly. "Both my father and brother are strategic players. They'll try to distance themselves and their practice from me, while still putting on a good public face."

She nodded, then grimaced. "Deviant Dentist? Who makes up this crap?"

He shrugged. All his life, his family had withstood public scrutiny. Fortunately he'd managed to stay out of the limelight, for the most part. The new nickname was the least of his troubles.

She crossed over to her briefcase and lifted out her laptop. "Well, let's get to work."

He drew his brows together. They'd both been awake all night, and it was now mid-morning. "Don't you want to sleep?" His body throbbed. Funnily, though, he remembered sensations, but not so much the actions. His brain was filled with a smoky haze when he tried to remember what he'd been doing before the news—a hot, sensual haze, but a haze nonetheless. He was injured, and he'd used a lot of his lightforce in trying to save Jared. Maybe he was simply exhausted. And horny.

She settled herself on the bed again, her dress hiking up to show a generous amount of curvy thigh, her computer on her lap as she started to read whatever was onscreen. "I'm a little wired, actually. I can do some work and catch a nap later." She didn't lift her gaze from the screen, but he saw the warm flush steal over her cheeks. She was aware of him, as much as he was aware of her, of the rumpled skirt of her dress showing off the curve of leg, of the torn bodice that would take little encouragement to fall from her shoulders ... he saw her look of intense concentration as she kept her gaze on the screen, but also noticed the jump in the pulse throbbing at the base of her throat. Yeah, she was aware of him, and fighting it.

"I need to rest, build up some energy," he told her quietly. He paused, then added, "There is one way I could recharge ..." he let his voice trail off suggestively as he eyed his sexy little lawyer.

She finally looked up, a single dark eyebrow arching in question. "And that is?"

He approached the bed and felt satisfaction when the curiosity in her gaze turned to awareness, tinged with a hot flash of desire. He bent and placed a palm on the violently coloured bedspread, close to her hip, and suddenly she wasn't so intent on her work.

"We could get to know each other better ...?" He leaned closer, angling his head to brush her cheek with his. So close, he could smell the spicy feminine fragrance she used, a hint of cinnamon with jasmine. He could also hear her breath hitch in her throat, see the muscles of her neck move as she swallowed.

He closed his eyes, opening his senses to hers, feeling the slow throb of arousal echo in her own body. It was enough to feed him a light flare of energy.

"Uh ... wh-what?" she stammered, her voice laced with a sexy little quiver. Damn, she was so responsive. He could imagine the energy burst if she'd just let him ...

"Let me give you pleasure," he whispered against her ear, biting the lobe gently. More energy, more light travelling through his senses, empowering him as she shuddered so delicately. He brushed his cheek against hers again, enjoying the sensation.

"Uh ..." Her hair brushed against his face, as though she was trying to shake off a trance. The movement, the caress of hair against skin, the scent ... an arc of desire shot through him, arousal hardening his body.

"Wait." She pulled back so she could meet his gaze. "You want to give me pleasure so you can 'rest and recharge'?"

He nodded, his body tightening at the mere suggestion.

She shook her head. "That has got to be the worst come-on I've ever heard." She turned back to her screen, her expression now aloof. "Try the old-fashioned way. Grab some shut-eye."

Just like that, his sexy lawyer switched from siren to professional in the blink of an eye.

He sighed. He could think of a quicker way to build up his energy stores, one that would be far more pleasurable than her going cross-eyed looking at reports and him getting a crick in the neck and God-only-knew-what from that filthy floor.

"As you wish," he sighed. He leaned over to grab a pillow beside her, sensed her muscles clench, the feminine arousal that arced through her, and smiled as he withdrew. She wasn't half as professionally distant as she'd have him believe.

"If you change your mind," he said softly as he settled himself on the floor, facing away from her. A secret smile spread across his face. He was a patient man.

"I won't."

His smile broadened as he felt her hot gaze on his body, and slowly drifted off to sleep.

* * *

Vassi gazed out of the windscreen, conscious of the big man next to her, yet trying to appear casual. Max had driven down a back road, and they were still two kilometres from the Alpine territory border.

"We'll have to hike in the rest of the way," he told her, and she nodded. Keep it professional. That episode in the hotel could not be repeated. He'd told her his story—yet still kept things hidden from her, as evidenced by the discovery of his connection to one of the wealthiest families in Irondell. A family he'd abandoned, dismissed, a family that just happened to be Marchetta's arch nemesis. And now she was defending one of them. Like that would go down well with her dream client. She couldn't deny the temptation to take Henley's advice and drop the case. Let this be someone else's headache. Yet she couldn't shake the memory of the lycans growling at the back of the courtroom, or the attack at Max's car. She had a responsibility, not only as an officer of the court, but as a truthseeker. All was not what it seemed with Jared's murder. Deep down, Max hadn't wanted the man dead. That much she could sense. That much she believed. Her conscience wouldn't let her drop the case, and yet by pursuing it she would burn any chance of representing the Marchetta family. That thought, the ramifications of taking on this case had kept her awake most of the day and into the night. Well, maybe that and the hot hunk with a gift for kissing sleeping on the floor beside her bed. That's what he had, a damn gift that would burn through the reserve of a chaste and devout nun.

Damn, she was tired. As a half-blood, her need for sleep was less than that of a human, but after spending the day gazing longingly at the sleeping hunk on the floor, her pathetic attempt at a nap had consisted of one hot, arousing fantasy after another—and next to no sleep. She'd woken that morning to find him watching over her, a glint in his eye that was at once protective and ... predatory.

And with a mostly healed shoulder, which just raised more questions he'd easily avoided.

"I'll call you if I find anything," she told him now as she shrugged into her white ski jacket. They'd found a clothing store in Summercliff that sold ex-hire ski clothes, and she'd used the company credit card to purchase suitable outfits for both of them, along with new underwear. By using company funds and not her own, it would be harder for the lycans to track her down—harder, but not impossible. She'd catch hell from the managing partners, but she'd smooth it over—later.

"What? You're not going in there alone." He reached into the backseat for his own jacket, but she placed her hand on his arm, stalling him. He'd pushed the long sleeves of his t-shirt back and her hand lay on his forearm, the muscles tightening beneath her fingertips at the contact. His scent, a musky male essence of sandalwood and something darker, sweeter, more elusive, surrounded her in the tight confines of the car. The sound of his deep voice, the smell of him, the feel of his skin beneath hers—he was one intensely attractive package. She had to remind herself: this was a client, and she never got involved with clients.

"You can't go in there, Max. The whole Alpine Pack is out for your blood. As soon as they get a whiff of your scent here, it will be like the hounds of hell descending upon us. I'm an officer of the court. I'm in tribal jurisdiction, but my office affords me some protection. I'll be fine."

"One: my name is Ryder. R.Y.D.E.R.," he spelled his name in a growl, and immediately a grey fog eclipsed his words in her mind. "Two: they attacked both of us just outside the police station," he pointed out, frowning. "What makes you think they won't hurt you if they catch you on their land? You're a vampire trespassing in werewolf territory."

"Ah, but I'm not trespassing. I'm preparing a legal defence. Until I'm asked to leave, it's not considered trespassing."

"It's too dangerous." His tone was clipped, abrupt.

"Only if you're with me." She shoved a couple of blood bank packs in her pocket for a high-energy snack later. He grasped her hand, and she finally met his gaze. His eyes showed his worry, his concern.

He cared for her safety, and the realisation warmed her. The memory of his confession still preoccupied her, though, along with thoughts on presenting his case in court. He felt some responsibility for the alpha prime's death, but she honestly didn't believe he was a murderer. She'd managed to get hold of the medical examiner's office that morning. A preliminary forensic report should be ready later today. Until then, there could be a number of explanations for Jared's death, including an unfortunate allergic reaction.

Max had no reason to kill the werewolf, but perhaps someone else did.

She turned her hand over to clasp his, enjoying the warmth, the strength inherent in his grip. "Trust me, I wouldn't do this if there was any other way. A half-blood vampire walking into werewolf territory—normally that would be a suicide march, but I have tribal law's protection. I can do this, don't worry."

"I don't like it," he said, his voice low and grating.

"I know. I'll be as quick as possible." She backed out of the car before she gave into temptation and crawled into the backseat with the attractive not-such-a-murderer. Who drove a hatchback. She shook her head as she tucked the map into her pocket, drew on her gloves and took off into the undergrowth.

When she was a good distance from the car, she paused beneath the overhanging fronds of a tree fern. The temperate rainforest was mainly wet and muddy, but the higher she trekked, the more snow she'd encounter, until she left the forest altogether. Now, the mountainside was eerily silent, the sun already beginning its descent past the peak. Her boot squelched in mud, and a cloud of white, thick fog was slowly descending. She wasn't sure if the low visibility would work for her or not.

She dug the map out of her pocket and surveyed it quickly. Territorial maps were notoriously inaccurate. Those who lived in the area knew it like the back of their paw, but they delighted in obscuring some hazards, even leaving some trails off the map entirely. No reason to give potential enemies access to secret roads and trails. Every tribe was like that, even some of the vampire colonies built in traps to the publicly released maps.

But the one trail that was always guaranteed to be accurate was the one leading to the reception hall. Strangers were afforded minimal access for trade and treaty or tribunal discussions. That's where she had to head. She could make public enquiries there as an officer of the law.

She folded the map and crammed it back into her pocket, gazing around the area as she rose to her feet. Not a bird tweeted. There was no scamper of critters' feet. A few hundred metres up the mountain was the end of the tree line and snow already covered the ground. She hoped the animals were simply in hibernation, and that there was no other reason for the creepy quiet.

She took off running, the trees and shrubs becoming a green-and-brown blur as she sped through the forest.

* * *

Ryder tapped his fingers on the steering wheel, then glanced at his watch. Okay, that was long enough. He'd given her a good hour's head start. Her arguments were sound—but he simply didn't like the idea of Vassiliki walking unprotected into a den of werewolves.

He slid out of the car, grabbed his jacket from the backseat, and hurriedly dressed. He was a light warrior. He didn't sit and wait.

He took off running in the direction Vassiliki had gone, consciously morphing his body's outline. He dispersed light particles around his body, effectively becoming invisible as he ran. It didn't take him long to pick up Vassiliki's trail and he sped up in pursuit, a wavering shape that blended into his surroundings.

* * *

Vassi paused under a rocky outcrop. Her breath misted in front of her. It was freezing. She'd left the tree line a while ago, and it was a hard slog through the deep snowdrifts. Even for a half-blood vampire, this place was cold. She unscrewed the cap of one of the blood packs and sucked on the fluid inside.

She swallowed thoughtfully, enjoying the metallic taste as it washed down her throat. She didn't need to find Jared's killer. She just needed to provide reasonable doubt. Unfortunately, Max's case didn't look so good. By his own admission, his actions directly caused the death of the alpha prime, no matter how unintended. Jared died in his surgery, under treatment. The crime lab could only detect Ryder's fingerprints on any of the tools involved, on the mixing pot and the adhesive jar. Even the werewolf sniffer team hadn't been able to detect any other contact.

But what if Ryder was just a tool? A mechanism for murder? Who stood to gain from Jared's death? She scrunched the blood pack and placed it inside a zip lock bag. She didn't want any wolves tracking the smell of fresh blood.

She dug a narrow, deep hole in the snow and buried the rubbish. She wasn't too far from the reception hall. She hoped to be in and out by nightfall.

She started to jog across the snowy mountain, bracing her hand occasionally against the steep rocky surface. She tried to do so sparingly—each contact was a scent point for a werewolf tracker. She was almost at the mouth of Howling Chasm when the snow exploded in front of her as a white wolf landed mere centimetres from the toes of her boots. She could feel his warm breath across her face as he bared his teeth in a snarl.

Chapter Five

Vassi froze, but couldn't help the reflexive lengthening of her own fangs. "I'm an officer of the court," she stated, keeping her voice calm, her eyes lowered to the furry chest of the wolf. Sunlight glinted on something around his neck, but she didn't bother to try and figure out what was hidden by his fur coat. She didn't want to provoke him. "I request permission to approach tribal reception."

The wolf prowled around her. Vassi remained still, her eyes on the disturbed snow in front of her as he brushed past her. He sniffed her, and she pursed her lips. Wolves liked to try and intimidate visitors. They invaded personal space, their presence intentionally domineering. She eventually swung her head around to glare at him. She'd dealt with many criminals, some of them very real monsters. She refused to be intimidated.

"Finished?"

The wolf nudged her, his snout shoving her between her shoulder blades. She plodded on through the snow with her silent, menacing escort. Every now and then he would stop and sniff the air, surveying the area around them with a wary stare, but each time he would eventually resume the journey.

* * *

Nearly an hour later, Vassi entered the Alpine Pack reception hall. It was a long narrow space cut into the side of the mountain. Lanterns hung from hooks lodged in the stone wall, casting a warm glow in some spots, leaving dark shadows in others. Sofas and seating nooks were placed along the edge of the hall, and several men and women lazed around, talking quietly—until they noticed her. Eventually, all conversation stopped.

The wolf at her side morphed, and a tall, broad-shouldered man with short white-blond hair stood beside her, naked but for a chain around his neck that bore a smooth, gold ring. The pendant rested against his tanned, muscled chest. He took her arm and led her up the length of the hall, casually catching the pair of trousers that were thrown his way.

When they reached the dais at the end, he pulled her to a stop. She kept her eyes straight ahead, ignoring him as he pulled the trousers on and zipped them. She couldn't ignore the fact that he didn't bother to button the fly, nor grab a shirt. Werewolves were notorious for being comfortable in their own skin and ... fit. This one was very, very ... fit.

The main chair on the dais swung round, and a woman with long, tawny blond hair stared down at her. Her eyes narrowed.

"Where is your client?"

So they knew who she was. Could this be the alpha's mate who'd attacked her and Max at his car? She tried to hide her surprise. It was highly unusual for an alpha prime's mate to step into the role of acting alpha—but then, again, she'd seen the she-wolf in action. The bitch could definitely fight.

"He's not here, if that's what you're asking. I come on a fact-finding mission. As an officer of the court, I respectfully request treaty in the Alpine tribal jurisdiction." Hopefully the banner of the court would provide enough protection in this werewolves' den.

The she-wolf bared her teeth, her eyes glowing. "You dare to request treaty, when you are defending the man who killed our alpha prime?" The words emerged from deep within her throat, almost as a growl.

"My client claims he didn't murder your alpha."

Several growls emanated from the hall, but she kept her gaze fixed on the woman on the dais. She cocked her head, and Vassi could see the gleam of curiosity as the glow in her eyes slowly banked.

"Who are you?"

"My name is Vassiliki Verity. I'm a lawyer."

"She's a vamp," the man next to her stated, his lip curling in distaste.

"Half-blood," she corrected him. He was a big man, even by lycan standards, with defined muscles and a scar across his ridged abdomen. She remembered the scars of the man she'd left behind. The lycan was attractive, but it was her client's body she wanted to stroke. Seraphina, on the other hand, would be all over this lycan in a blink. She turned back to the woman on the dais. "And you?"

"I am Samantha."

Jared's partner. Getting information from the Alpine wolves suddenly seemed much more difficult. That darn grey fog descended over the words again. "You strike me more as a Diana," Vassi said, and the woman growled. She didn't even move her lips, but the sound was clear in its warning.

The she-wolf leaned forward in her chair, her eyes narrowing as she sniffed the air.

"You've lain with him," she stated, her tone accusing.

Damn. She'd had a shower before they left, but apparently it wasn't enough to rid his scent. "Not ... quite." They'd kissed on the bed, but that was it. She was trying to stay professional.

The man next to her nodded. Great. So he'd known exactly who she was when he jumped out at her.

"We've kissed." There was no point in denying it, and she wanted them to see her as cooperative, not deceitful.

"You came into Alpine territory," 'Diana' stated. She tilted her head. "What did you hope to achieve?"

"My client didn't intend for your partner to die," Vassi stated clearly. "But somebody else may have. I'm here to find out who would have a reason for wanting Jared dead."

This time the growls from the crowd in the reception hall were louder.

The she-wolf leaned back in her chair and slowly crossed her legs. "Nobody here wanted Jared dead," she stated coldly.

Vassi slid her hand inside her jacket, and froze when her wrist was grabbed by the tall lycan next to her. He glared at her, his green gaze suspicious. She slowly withdrew her hand, his grip still on her wrist, and showed him the vial of lipstick.

He arched a blond eyebrow, then slowly relinquished her.

"How long were you and Jared mated?" Vassi asked as she casually applied her lipstick, then smacked her lips. She liked to be prepared.

"Not long enough," the woman said, her eyes taking on a sadness that Vassi could tell was sincere. "Two years." The woman's mournful longing was almost tangible to Vassi, her truthseeking gift sensing her melancholy as well as her honesty.

"I understand this was Jared's first visit to this particular surgery. Why didn't he go to your usual dentist?"

The she-wolf's glance flicked to the lycan beside her, then darted away. Vassi pursed her lips. Please be honest. She was reluctant to kiss the she-wolf in search of the truth.

The woman on the dais sighed. "He didn't want everyone to know of his problem. He saw it as a sign of weakness."

Vassi frowned. "Miscreants need teeth replaced all the time. Werewolves, cats, bears—even vampires. I don't understand why he would view it as a weakness."

The woman tilted her head back, her tawny hair falling over one shoulder. "Then you don't know the Alpine Pack, half-blood," she said dryly. "We are the strongest—we have to be, to live where we do," she said in an unconscious gesture to the snowfields beyond the wall of the mountain. "It was a matter of pride for Jared. If he was going to need a false tooth, it had to be as strong, if not stronger than his own."

"Why didn't he go to your pack's normal dentist? Why try a new one?"

Diana folded her arms. "Our dentist is not exclusive. Jared wouldn't have been able to go there without others seeing."

"Others? Who was Jared afraid of seeing him there?"

The woman's teeth bared as she placed her hands on the armrests of her chair. "Jared wasn't afraid of anything, or anyone." The words were spoken in a low, husky rumble. "He was doing it to protect the pack."

Vassi's frown deepened. How would a visit to the dental surgery put his pack at risk? Everyone needed to go sooner or later, it wasn't really considered a weakness. Had Diana another motive?

"Did you want him dead?"

She could feel the glare of the lycan next to her, but kept her attention on the she-wolf. Anger flared in the woman's eyes, although her pose remained relaxed. Her hand dropped to her stomach in a protective gesture, as though to ward off Vassi's barbs.

"No, I did not."

Vassi sensed warmth emanating from the woman. There was no chill of deceit or prevarication, no omission. Just a tonne of regret and sadness. Jared's mate had not been involved with his death. There was something else, though, something the woman wasn't going to share with her. Vassi could sense another's essence, just the tiniest flare of warmth. The she-wolf would bear a pup in the spring, all the more reason for her not to be involved in her mate's murder. Unfortunately, Jared's death would have a ripple effect through the generations of the Alpine pack.

Vassi nodded. "I apologise. In my line of work I have to ask some tough questions, and there's rarely a nice way to go about it. Would you mind if I asked your tribe some questions?" She held up a hand at the woman's frown. "I promise to keep it brief, and then I'll be on my way." She needed the acting alpha's permission before interviewing anyone in the tribe's territory.

The she-wolf reluctantly nodded, her expression impatient.

Vassi eyed the lycan beside her. "And you are?"

He cocked his head, glancing around the room, a line marring his brow. His fists clenched, shoulders back, his chest rose as he breathed in slowly. For a moment Vassi thought he was going to ignore her completely, although she knew that he was keeping track of her with a heightened level of awareness.

Finally he turned his head to look at her. "Matthias."

She waited for the mental fog to rise and roll over the name. Her eyebrows rose as his name remained with a crystal clarity in her mind. "Oh. It suits you," she commented. Matthias blinked at the remark.

"Matthias is—was Jared's guardian prime." Diana's voice caught on her words.

Vassi nodded. "Ah. So, with Jared's death, perhaps you now have an opportunity to become alpha prime?" She knew the question was blunt, even offensive. She also knew that using the element of shock made it more difficult for subjects to mask their reactions.

Matthias, though, surprised her. His expression remained cool, remote, as he shook his head. "No."

Vassi waited, but the lycan didn't seem inclined to chitchat. "No? The pack will need a new alpha. Why not you?"

"I don't wish to be alpha," he said, his voice low. He was losing patience, not enjoying having to explain himself. "I have no desire to replace Jared. He was my friend, and I respected him. I won't take his place."

Vassi frowned. The waves washing over her ran hot and cold, like diving into a pool at the beginning of summer and finding the warm spots as you swam a lap. It was confusing;

she couldn't pull apart where the deceit was, and what was said in all honesty. She did know that he wasn't about to share the information willingly.

She reached for him, her movements lightning fast. She saw his brief look of surprise when she grasped his head and pulled him down for a kiss, reaching out with her gift.

Her lips met his, and she gasped at the warm contact. He was like a wall of heat. He may have been surprised by her move, but his reaction was quick. He slid his tongue inside her mouth and took command of the kiss, melding her body to his, the ring around his neck pressing into the spot between her breasts.

She tore her lips from the lycan, breathless but still in control. Interesting. The guy was a great kisser, but apparently she preferred her men scarred and on the wrong side of the law.

"Do you want to be alpha prime?" she murmured rapidly to the lycan as he blinked, fighting the compulsion. She fed a little more of her gift through their connection. His eyes finally glazed over. She'd only have a few minutes before the other lycans stepped in to stop their conversation.

"I can't. I am not of the Alpine Pack, I have no claim." The answer was a low rumble as she compelled him to answer.

She frowned. He hadn't quite answered the question—odd. "Do you want to be alpha?" she repeated, strengthening her words with her gift.

"Yes," he murmured, his green gaze ablaze as he fought against the yoke of her gift. This one fought the compulsion, a shock as every other creature succumbed easily. This lycan, though, seemed entirely aware of her attempt to control him. "But because I'm worthy, not because I failed the man I'd sworn to protect. I cannot claim Alpha Prime for Alpine Pack. You're not born an alpha, you have to earn it." His words came back at her with heat and more. His honesty was brutal in its effect, and she gritted her teeth against the sensations bombarding her, battering her with his sincerity, pain and a dark determination.

"Did you want Jared dead?"

"No. Jared took me into his pack. I am completely loyal to him. I will serve his pack until a new prime is decided." His commitment to the pack, to his friend, was harsh and unyielding. Alpine Pack's guardian prime was resolute in his protection of his adopted pack. It was obvious the lycan felt a deep sense of guilt over the death of the alpha prime, but not because he'd had anything to do with it, rather that he hadn't been able to prevent it. Now she understood the ambivalence she'd sensed before.

"Who would benefit from Jared's death?" She sensed the she-wolf shifting in her chair, impatient for their conversation to end.

"Nobody in the pack has a clear track to prime position," Matthias stated calmly, and Vassi nodded. Usually challengers fought the alpha to obtain the prime position. If the alpha prime had died, though, all male wolves fought through rounds of challenges until the final winner was awarded the prime's position. A level playing field to ensure the leader was the pack's strongest.

"Outsiders? Who are your pack enemies?"

"Woodland Pack, and Southside Colony."

Vassi nodded. She knew of some of the conflict with Woodland Pack, had seen enough cases in the courtroom to know that there was some serious trouble from that quarter. Satisfied she'd gotten the information she needed, she severed the connection.

Matthias blinked, his eyes slowly losing their unfocused look. He frowned down at her, slowly sliding his hands from around her waist to step back. "What did you just do to me?"

She waved a nonchalantly. "Oh, that's just a custom where I come from. You know, when we give our condolences." It was amazing how easily lies sprang to her own lips.

He narrowed his eyes. "You play dirty." He knew exactly what she'd been doing. This was a strong alpha, not easily fooled. She'd need to remember that for any future dealings. She'd been surprised he'd resisted the compulsion earlier. That he remembered while supposedly under a fog showed a strength of mind she hadn't encountered before. But for now, he'd been honest, and wasn't party to Jared's death.

"Be thankful I'm only playing." She turned to the woman on the dais. "Thank you for your cooperation. I formally request that Alpine Pack recognise the court's jurisdiction over my client, and to ward off action until the trial is decided."

The lycan next to her growled, low and dangerous, but she kept her gaze on the she-wolf. The woman smirked.

"You expect us to back off? My mate died in his surgery. We won't back off."

Vassi pursed her lips. Well, it had been worth a try. "You can't enforce tribal law if the court has already established jurisdiction," she reminded the woman gently. Her client was facing trial—the tribes had to respect the process, despite their need to spill blood.

"Then you'd better work fast. If your client is as innocent as he claims," the woman said softly, "then you'd better prove it. Justice will be served, one way or another."

"Is that a threat?"

"It's a promise."

* * *

Ryder clenched his fists as he watched from the tree line. He was still in full veil, cloaking himself in the shreds of light, masking his presence. The white wolf stopped at the edge of the snow, sitting on his haunches. The lycan sniffed the air, and for a moment he thought the wolf could actually see him, his gaze zeroing in on his position, but the wolf's gaze eventually moved on.

Vassiliki trudged behind him, her dark hair a stark contrast to the snow. She paused next to the wolf and looked about enquiringly. The wolf nudged her along, pressing against her with a shoulder before sitting again. The muscles in Ryder's jaw clenched as he ground his teeth.

She'd kissed the mutt.

He'd seen and heard everything, creeping into the wolves' den under his mantle of dispersed light. He'd witnessed her 'interrogation', and it had taken considerable restraint not to walk up to the kissing couple and tear them apart. Only the fact that he was outnumbered, and by revealing his presence would put his amorous lawyer at risk held him back— although God only knew why he'd felt so … jealous. She was his lawyer, damn it. Not his girlfriend. He watched now through narrowed eyes as she kept walking, leaving the wolf behind her. He'd been so worried about her, so damn anxious over her safety. She'd seemed quite comfortable in the werewolves' den. Her breath gusted in front of her as she trudged toward the cover of the trees. Not once did she look back at the wolf who watched her.

She passed within inches of his spot, oblivious to his presence, which just rankled him further, although God only knew why. He followed her, then paused when he heard the growl behind him. He glanced over his shoulder. The wolf had tracked his movement. Perhaps he'd made a sound, or his movement had drawn attention to his blurred outline. Either way, the wolf now stood an all paws, teeth bared, erect ears pointing forward.

Ryder smiled, but it wasn't friendly. He was in wolf territory, he was prey, but given the opportunity, he'd definitely take this wolf on. He met the wolf's gaze, and relaxed his control over his light so that he could be seen, ever so briefly.

The wolf growled, low and deep, and took a menacing step forward, then another. A twig snapped deep in the woods, and Ryder hoped it was Vassiliki. The white wolf froze, angled his head and listened.

After a moment he returned his gaze to Ryder and lifted his snout, as though gesturing after the sexy vamp, before turning and bounding back across the snow. Ryder frowned. He'd been expecting a fight. Hell, was hoping for one, but the wolf had turned and …

A howl echoed from deep within the forest, and Ryder's head whipped around. Damn. Neither he nor Vassiliki had been bothered on the way up to Alpine territory, but the forest belonged to Woodland Pack, and they were on the hunt.

Vassiliki.

Chapter Six

Ryder took off running, his feet silent as he pelted through the forest, jumping over bushes and fallen logs, ducking low-hanging branches, his eyes on the tracks Vassiliki had left in the muddy soil. It had been years since he'd done a forest hunt, but after working with miscreants on a constant basis, his skills were still well-honed.

The footprints were becoming deeper and further apart. She'd started running. He lengthened his own stride, trying to figure out how much of a start she had on him. More howling echoed through the forest. More wolves were taking up the cry. They were hunting Vassiliki. No way was he letting his sexy little vamp come to harm. She was under his protection, whether she realised it or not, and he couldn't let any harm come to her. One woman on his conscience was one too many, he couldn't stand it if that number rose to two.

He vaulted over a log and skidded as he rounded a bend. There. He could see a blur of white moving through the trees. Damn, she was fast. He left the trail, cutting cross-country to make up time and distance. Her hair trailed behind her, her arms slicing through the air as she ran with the speed and grace of a sprinter in hyper drive. He could hear the wolves running toward them as he jumped and raced down the side of the mountain, taking the shorter, more perilous route to catch up with his lawyer.

Woodland Pack. They were a wild bunch, notorious for territorial disputes and a general disregard for boundaries, rules and governance of any kind. They wouldn't respect Vassiliki's claim for treaty as an officer of the court—if they gave her the time to form the request. He rounded a tree, the flash of her white jacket so close. He launched himself, tackling her to the ground.

They fell and rolled, soundless in the woods as she fought him off. She didn't scream, she didn't yell—she just fought silently, her talons appearing to slice through the outer lining of his jacket as she tried to buck him off. He clapped a hand over her mouth, wincing when her fangs pricked his palm. He stared into her glowing eyes that were shifting from brown to gold to blood red as she tasted his blood—until she caught his scent, and realisation slowly banked the glow in her eyes to an angry gold. Her talons retracted.

He shifted and rolled, dragging her under the overhanging fronds of a tree fern. He settled himself over her again, using his body to shield hers, extending his veil to cover the vamp beneath him, despite her attempt to shove him off and wriggle out.

He held a finger to his lips, his other hand still covering her mouth as the pad of paws thundered down the path. Werewolves came bounding through the trees, and he peered through the fern fronds. They were searching for them, noses to the ground. He counted four. Guardians, he could tell. They were all slightly larger than the average wolf, built for strength and stamina. They were the boundary wardens, guarding the territory against intrusion. Skilled in the hunt.

Vassiliki was still beneath him, her wide-eyed gaze on the wolves. He waited patiently. As long as they were still, the wolves wouldn't find them, no matter how close they came to their hiding spot, no matter where their scent trail led them.

In full veil, even his scent was blurred, spreading out and around to seem more like a faint cloud than a strong trail. Using his body to shield Vassiliki's covered her scent, also.

After a while the wolves howled, frustration evident in their cries, before they trotted off in several directions.

Ryder didn't relax until he was certain they were alone. He dipped his head to touch his forehead to Vassiliki's and sighed. Great. They were in Woodland territory, and guardians were hunting them. Well, hunting the alpha-killing dentist, anyway. Vassiliki would be collateral damage.

If they could just get back to Blanche, they could drive back into Summercliff, which was outside the Woodland boundary. He tried to clear his mind, tried to think rationally of the next thing to do, but the soft body beneath his proved too much of a distraction. Her breasts were crushed beneath his chest and his thighs straddled her hips, his groin against hers.

He should get up. He was probably crushing her. He shifted his head to gaze down at her and saw the unmistakable flare of desire in her now-golden gaze. He hardened against her, heard the hitch in her breath as she felt his arousal, her cinnamon scent teasing at him. He wanted to rock against her, to lick the alabaster skin of her neck, feel her arch beneath him—like she had on the hotel bed.

He blinked at the memory that burst through a fog, of them kissing on the bed, and her asking him questions—just like she'd done with the lycan.

He heaved himself off her, his body screaming in denial. "We should go," he told her roughly as he rose. He reached down for her, grasping her hand and pulling her easily to her feet, her eyes still golden with desire as she held on to him.

She finally dropped her gaze to their clasped hands. She turned his hand over in hers, sliding the other across his skin in a soft caress, then pouted when she saw the cuts she'd made with her fangs when he'd covered her mouth.

For a moment, his gaze was held by that mouth, those lips pursed in the perfect position for a kiss. She lowered her head slowly and flicked her tongue out to lave the wounds. Like an arrow to his groin, desire shot through his body, hot, hard and damn near uncontrollable as the sexy little vampire licked his wounds. Her pink tongue darted out, and his skin tingled wherever she touched him, her gaze never leaving his as she wove an erotic spell around him.

Hard as a rock, he wanted to pull her back down onto the sweet earth and torment her with the same wicked attention—but he wouldn't stop at her hand. He wanted to lick her all over. She avoided his grasp and let go of his hand.

"You're right," she said huskily. Her chest rose beneath the white parka. He wanted to rip it off her, frustrated by its ability to mask her body from his gaze. "We should go, before the guardians return."

She took off jogging, like a white ghost lost in the trees. For a moment he stood there, gaping, his hand still raised, the cool breeze dancing across and chilling his skin where she'd left her delicate kisses. The small wounds were already healing, a warm sensation spreading up his arm—and down to his groin. He could barely walk, damn it.

But she was right, they were in the middle of a forest with a small army of wolves hunting them. He took off at an uncomfortable jog. He hated that she was right. Hated that she'd so easily wrung a reaction from his body. Hated that he wasn't the only one she'd kissed, and hated himself for hating that.

* * *

Vassi kept her gaze on the screen, despite the temptation of watching Max dry himself with a towel, his jeans zipped but unfastened. She'd seen his reaction in the forest, had felt his arousal, and it had inflamed hers. She wasn't a prude, but she did have one rule—never get involved with a client. What she'd been tempted to do, what she'd been tempted to allow him to do—shouldn't be done. Period.

She opened up her email, keeping her gaze on her device as notices started to load. She immediately clicked on the medical examiner's preliminary report. Besides, the man had issues, aside from the glaring one of a murder charge hanging over his head. He'd left his family. She shook her head. That was so hard for her to wrap her brain around.

As a half-blood, she was one of those creatures with a foot in each tribe, but never really belonging in either. The vampire colony of her father didn't like the taint of human in her. She was seen as weak, her humanity an inescapable vulnerability. She wasn't subject to the same blood craving as her father's colony, wasn't driven by the need to slake her thirst for blood with the death of a human. She liked the taste of blood, and she did need it to survive, but she could also eat human food—bloodlust didn't drive her actions at the cost of another's life.

She'd long learned never to reveal her truthseeking abilities—either to her father's colony, or the humans of her mother's acquaintance. Truthseekers were viewed as intruders, trespassing through the consciousness without permission. Nobody wanted others to know when they were concealing the truth, nobody liked to be exposed in that way—and many would kill to keep their secrets safe.

On the other hand, her mother's family treated her existence with the same shame and disappointment as a divorce in the Catholic Church eons ago, before the Reformation. Some of them acknowledged her, but most treated her as though they expected her to go all blood-crazy on them and attack. There were some, though, a very special few, who treated her with respect. She hoped one day that would grow to acceptance, maybe even love. Until then, she had her work to keep her busy, to keep her company at night and on family holidays.

For Max to just discard his family, one that had apparently accepted and approved of him, went against everything that Vassi held dear. If she had a family who acknowledged her, who welcomed her—possibly even loved her—there was no way she would abandon them.

Max strolled back into the bathroom, and her gaze followed his movement, that sexy shoulder roll thing he did when he moved drawing her focus. He reminded her of some of the cats she'd seen in nightclubs, the graceful motion of their body to their own hidden rhythm. He had broad shoulders, well-muscled with smooth, golden skin. His back was just as gorgeous as his front. Her gaze dropped to his jeans. That butt ... she sighed. No, she didn't get involved with clients.

He hung up the towel on the rail then turned, meeting her gaze. He paused in the doorway, leaning against the jamb. Her mouth dried. His chest, his stomach, all bore the ridged proof of his strength. He looked like a calendar pin-up, lounging in the bedroom with a challenging glint to his gaze. God, she wanted to get involved with her client.

"What did you learn from the Alpine wolves?" he asked, his deep timbre rolling over her body, building an awareness she was trying very hard to ignore. His gaze was intent. He hadn't really spoken since they'd left the forest, keeping his own counsel as he'd driven that cramped little car back down to the motel in Summercliff. She'd been too intent on trying to get control of her body, squelching her arousal so that she could pretend to be cool, calm and collected. She briefly wondered why his curiosity had taken so long to surface. Then she wondered what the hell he'd been doing in the forest when he was supposed to be waiting for her in the car, how he could appear out of nowhere, or how four guardians could possibly have missed them. She was hesitant to ask though. She didn't want him to lie to her, not again.

"I don't believe anyone there is responsible for the alpha's death," she told him. "His mate is pregnant. She had no reason to want him dead. In fact, she had a very important reason for him to remain alive."

Max nodded. "I see. What about the others?" he asked casually, levering himself away from the jamb and walking over to the chair where she'd draped her ski jacket.

"The others?" she watched him move, enjoying the play of the lamplight over his golden skin.

"Yeah, you know, the one you kissed."

She blinked. "How did you—you saw that?" She shook her head. She hadn't seen him in the den. How had he known?

"Yeah. I did." He reached for her jacket and she rose from the bed as he pulled the lipstick vial out of the pocket. "I saw everything," he told her, holding up the case as he arched an eyebrow.

"Then you know what he said," she murmured, her heart beating faster. She reached for the vial, but he raised it above his head. She didn't like anybody else handling her stuff. She didn't want anybody to guess her other skills—that was too dangerous. "How could you see? Where were you?" It was inconceivable that such a big man could sneak into the heart of a wolves' den without being discovered. No wonder Matthias had been sniffing like a flu-struck dog. He must have caught some of Max's scent.

"I didn't like that you went in there without protection, so I followed you."

"Are you mad? Do you know what could have happened if you'd been caught?" She frowned. He'd taken such a risk.

"But I didn't get caught," he said quietly. He turned the vial in his hand. "Interesting. Yesterday I wanted to crawl onto that bed and make love to you, and I couldn't remember how I got to that point."

She swallowed. He was guessing, surely. He couldn't know—not for sure. She tamped down on the wave of panic, trying to retain some calm, some control. Nobody could know.

She tried to laugh, to dismiss his remarks. "That's hardly flattering. Wanting to make love to me and not knowing why." She raised an eyebrow. "Or is it the how that escapes you?" She was being deliberately provocative, she knew. Anything to divert his attention, to make him focus on something other than her lipstick, and what happened when she used it.

She folded her arms in front of her, feeling the raised ridges of skin on the side of her abdomen through her clothes. Nobody could know.

His eyelids lowered, his gaze sliding to her, and suddenly she was breathless. That look, that wicked, knowing, seductive look, promised all sorts of dark, dangerous things. "Oh, I can figure out the how, trust me," he said, his voice low. "But I'm interested as to how I could kiss a woman and completely forget about it."

Well, darn. How did she respond to that? Just leaving his remark alone stung her ego. Damn it, if she kissed him without the truth serum, he'd bloody well remember it—not that she could tell him, though, because then she'd have to admit to using the truth serum.

"I don't know what you're talking about," she said, lifting her chin at her lie.

"Is it because your kisses are so unremarkable, they're easily forgotten?" Now he was being deliberately provocative, damn it. She pursed her lips.

"I kissed a lycan." She shrugged. "Big deal."

"But then he couldn't remember much of it, either." His voice was low, silky as he thought aloud. "I wonder why that is?"

She trembled, and she tightened her arms around herself for a moment until she realised how defensive the posture made her seem. She put her hands on her hips in an attempt to brazen it out.

"I really have no idea what you're talking about. Besides, last I looked you were my client, Max. Not my keeper." She glanced over her shoulder to the laptop sitting on the bed. "We should get back to work, the ME's report is in."

He slid his arm around her waist, dragging her up against his body. She blinked, stunned at the quick move. For a human, he was fast—fast enough to surprise her.

"Ryder," he whispered, his mouth close to hers. "Not Max. Ryder. Why is it you can never remember my name, Vassi, and I can't remember your kiss?"

Chapter Seven

She noticed his shortening of her name a split second before his mouth met hers, and all her buried desire flared anew, consuming her as his lips slanted across hers. She really should stop this. Put the guy in his place. She opened her mouth beneath his, and his tongue slid in, playing with hers in a sensual game of kiss-chasey. Soon. She'd stop him soon. She slid her hands up his arms, enjoying the definition of biceps as he pulled her even closer, before wrapping her arms around his neck.

She moaned as her breasts pressed against his chest, her nipples tightening as sensation after sensation bombarded her. Heat—so much tantalising heat that made her want to crawl inside his skin and revel in it. He cupped her butt, lifting her up against him, and she moaned at his display of strength as she wrapped her legs around him. Separated by two layers of denim, he rubbed his cock, long and hard against the juncture of her thighs, and a liquid heat seeped into her panties at the contact.

He backed her up against the dresser, letting her rest on the top as he continued to kiss her with a skill that left her hot and breathless and oh-so-willing. His hands cradled her face, angling her head for a deeper kiss. She moaned again, arching against him. So warm, everything was so warm. Her nipples were tight, hard nubs, and she rubbed them against his chest, her hips meeting his thrusts as they writhed against each other, the furniture knocking against the wall.

She wasn't sure how long her phone rang for before she noticed the intrusion. Max grew still at the sound, then lifted his mouth from hers, locking his gaze with hers.

She swallowed. "I have to get that."

He scooped her up from the dresser, then let her body slide down his frame until her feet touched the floor.

"Then I guess you'd better get it," he said, letting go of her.

She walked over to her bag on the bed on shaky legs, almost ripping her handbag in frustration as she yanked her phone out of its depths. She was equal parts relieved and angry at the interruption.

"Yes?" she said, breathless, holding the phone to her ear as she gazed back at Max.

He now leaned against the dresser, arms folded across his bare, muscled chest, looking quite calm and in control, damn it.

She brushed her hair over her shoulder as she tried to regulate her breathing.

"Vassi? Are you all right?"

Seraphina. Not for the first time, her assistant's timing sucked. "Yeah, Seraphina. What's up?"

"You sound out of breath—oh, my God, am I interrupting something?" The woman squealed the words out. Vassi winced as she pulled the phone away from her ear for a moment.

"No, it's fine. What's the matter?"

"I did, didn't I? Is he as hot and wild as he looks? Tell me he is."

Vassi pursed her lips. "Did you need something, Seraphina?" She refused to indulge her friend's curiosity.

"Oh, I always need something. Hot, hard and—"

"Seraphina," Vassi interrupted briskly, "you rang me …"

"Has he got a mighty wang? He looks like the type."

Heat flushed across Vassi's cheeks, and she saw curiosity flare in Max's eyes briefly before she turned to hide her embarrassment. She was still flushed and warm—and yes, aroused. And she was having an entirely inappropriate conversation about a client—who stood within earshot.

"I'm hanging up—"

Seraphina tsked. "Oh, see, you're cranky. That's what happens when you deprive your magic hoo-hah of a mighty wang."

Vassi covered her eyes. "Good lord, sometimes you can be such a juvenile," she muttered into the phone. "Was there a purpose to this call, Seraphina?"

"Oh, yes. The medical examiner's report is in—have you seen it yet?"

"Haven't had a chance to read it yet."

"I'll save you some of the frustration of deciphering the mumbo jumbo. Jared Gray was poisoned."

Vassi stilled. "Really? How?" She was so conscious of the man behind her, it was as though her body had locked in on him like a homing beacon.

"Wolfsbane was added to a vial of adhesive in your client's surgery. The dose was toxic enough to kill several wolves. Very concentrated, very rare."

"I see." Wolfsbane had no effect on vampires, and in concentrated doses it could kill humans, but the creatures most susceptible to its effects were the wolves and other shifters. The alpha prime had been poisoned intentionally.

"Oh, and one more thing," Seraphina began, her voice a low, conspiratorial whisper. Vassi could just picture her hunkering down behind the reception desk, gazing around the office like a spy. "You need to move. RB was in the accounts department when your credit card charge came through. She knows where you are, and I wouldn't be surprised if she's sent out a posse of pack mates to track that Lord of Hotness you're shagging."

"We're not sha—" she bit the rest of her response off, supremely conscious of the man listening in on her side of the conversation.

"Out of everything I just said, you focused on that. Interesting. Like I said though, you need to scram. I think she also contacted Ms. Marchetta. Oops, gotta go, there's a gorgeous vampire stepping out of the lift."

Vassi stared blankly at the phone, the dial tone mocking her before she finally pressed the call off button.

"What was that about?"

The deep voice spurred her into action. The man had poisoned Jared Gray. She forced herself to remember their previous discussion, to cling to the belief of his innocence. He may have poisoned the alpha prime, but perhaps not intentionally. And werewolves knew where to find them. "We need to leave. Now."

She hurried over to the bed and snapped her laptop closed, shoving it into her briefcase. She scooped up her torn clothes from the previous day and shoved them into the shopping bag they'd used for their new purchases.

"What's happened?" Max's voice was muffled as he pulled his t-shirt on over his head.

"Someone in my office has leaked our location. We need to get out of here before any guests arrive."

Max quickly grabbed any items lying around the room, stuffing them into the bag, then grasped her arm and tugged her toward the door.

"Wait," he said, pulling her back behind him. He opened the door a little and peered out. He took his time, surveying the street, eyes narrowed. He frowned and pulled back, shutting the door.

"What? What's the matter?" Vassi asked.

"We already have company. Come on," he said, and crossed to the bathroom. Vassi grimaced. There wasn't even a window in there. The motel room's windows fronted onto the veranda, which fronted on to the parking lot. They were sitting ducks.

"Maybe I can go and talk to them, negotiate safe passage," she suggested. Max snorted as he lowered the toilet seat and stepped on top of it.

"They're not here to talk, Vassi."

He pressed a portion of the ceiling tiles up and shifted it to the side. Vassi gaped at the narrow hole.

"Uh, what are you doing?" Did he really expect her to climb through that?

"We have about a minute before they figure out which room we're in," he said, reaching over to pull the strap of her briefcase off her shoulder. He slid the case up into the cavity, then beckoned to her.

She grimaced, then stepped up onto the toilet lid. He braced one foot on the vanity, then interlocked his fingers, creating a stirrup for her to step into. She shot him a dubious look, and he jerked his chin.

"Hurry up."

She put her foot into his hands, braced a hand on his shoulder and stepped up.

"Ups-a-daisy," he muttered, and lifted her. She grabbed the sides of the hole and pulled herself through, then crawled along the struts of the ceiling. She rolled away as Max's hands braced along the rim of the tiles and he pulled himself through, angling his body to slide in along panels. He quickly replaced the tile as she heard wood break under the force of a kick.

The lycans had arrived.

* * *

Ryder held a finger to his lips, then gestured for Vassiliki to crawl in front of him. From his memory of the motel layout, there were three rooms between theirs and the end of the block. Fortunately the roof cavity was one combined space between the ground and first floors, and he commando-crawled along until he found the manhole into the last unit.

The cavity was hot, all the heaters in the units cranked up against the chill of the oncoming evening.

He could hear the lycans tearing apart their room. It wouldn't be long before they figured out what they'd done. They needed to move quickly. He placed his ear against the tile and listened. When he was satisfied the unit was empty, he slid the tile aside, dangled his feet through the gap and dropped silently down to the bathroom floor. He caught the briefcase Vassiliki dropped down to him, then grabbed her legs and guided her through, enjoying the feel of her body against his, albeit briefly.

Finger to lips, he hurried her to the door. He cracked it open a bit, and saw the one lycan standing guard further down the veranda. He wasn't doing much of a job of it, though, as he turned to see what his pack mates were doing inside the unit. Ryder opened the door and slid out, pulling Vassiliki behind him, her bag slung over his shoulders. He quickly dragged her around the corner of the building and halted, quickly scanning the parking lot.

They wouldn't get far on foot, not with wolves chasing them. He'd parked Blanche close to the exit—another car had been parked in their spot when they'd arrived back from their jaunt up the mountain. He pursed his lips. They might just be able to make it.

He ran from one car to the next, using them as cover, keeping the vehicles between them and the motel rooms. Vassiliki was close on his heels.

He ducked down, feeling along the bottom rim of Blanche's chassis until he found the small magnet box. He grinned as he withdrew his spare key. It was old school, and not really a secure location, but as yet nobody had ever tried to steal his car, so the key was more for his convenience than anything else.

Still in a crouch, he inserted the key and turned, wincing at the slight click. He rose up to peer over the hood of the car.

The lycan standing guard turned.

For a moment their gazes met, then the man growled. Ryder yanked open the door and pushed Vassiliki in.

"Go, go, go."

She clambered over to the passenger seat as he slid in right behind her. The lycan started running, shifting into wolf form mid-stride as Ryder slammed the door shut.

He started Blanche, throwing the car into reverse as the wolf jumped up on the hood.

Ryder pulled the steering wheel to one side as he jerked up the parking brake, sending the car into a spin. The wolf fell off and rolled along the asphalt as Ryder slammed the car into drive and sped away. He didn't brake as he turned onto the street, ignoring the cars that skidded to avoid collision.

He glanced into the rear-vision mirror. The other lycans had raced out of the motel room and were piling into a black SUV. He swerved around a corner, jumping up over the kerb, tyres squealing as he turned the car in the direction of the highway.

"Where are we going?" Vassiliki asked tightly as she held on to the grip above the passenger door.

"Good question. Where can we go where the werewolves won't follow?"

"Hammerhead Ridge," she suggested, peering over her shoulder. "Oh, God, they're right behind us."

He took the ramp to the highway, slowing down just enough so as not to fly off the curve. "What's at Hammerhead Ridge?" he asked as he depressed the accelerator, increasing his speed as the ramp slowly straightened out. He was unfamiliar with the name. He checked the mirror. She was right. The lycans were right behind them.

"A vampire colony."

Ryder frowned. From a wolf den to a vampire nest. He wasn't quite sure which was worse. Venturing into a colony was different to just passing through territory. It would be like stringing a steak around his neck and wandering through a den. Human blood was their preferred meal.

"Any other suggestions?" The small car darted between the occasional vehicle, the lycans close behind them. The sky was darkening to a deep purple as the sun set, the darker mountain peaks like black sentinels against the skyline.

"No."

He jerked forward as the SUV slammed into them from behind. He swore as he struggled with the steering wheel as the car started to slide.

"Oh, my God, what are they thinking?" Vassiliki cried, glancing back out of the rear window. The SUV switched on its high beams, and Ryder ducked as the rear-vision mirror caught the reflection, blinking as he tried to avoid being blinded. He peered into the darkness beyond the windscreen.

"They're determined, I'll give them that."

The car jolted again, and he swore underneath his breath as he caught sight of Vassiliki's wide-eyed gaze. He could understand the lycans' anger, even felt responsible to a degree, but that was no reason to put his innocent companion at risk of her life. Weaving the car across the road to avoid traffic and the vehicle behind them, he was conscious of the guardrail, and the dark drop into oblivion beyond.

He checked the rear-vision mirror, the headlights growing larger as the SUV prepared to ram them again. He floored the accelerator, edging away at the last moment. He swerved, dodging another attempt, but wasn't fast enough when the SUV surged forward and rammed them on the right rear wheel well.

The car jack-knifed, skidding across the road. There was another jolt as the SUV rammed the car on the passenger side, and Vassiliki cried out. Ryder saw the guardrail speed up towards them through his side window, then there was a crunch, sparks, and suddenly they were airborne. Ryder flung his arm out to brace Vassiliki for impact as trees slammed up to meet them, branches cracking the windscreen. Glass flew, and Ryder turned his face away. His centre of gravity reversed as the car somersaulted down the ravine.

Chapter Eight

Vassi blinked. Everything was swimming and she bit back a wave of nausea. Damn, but she hurt. Her head lolled at an awkward angle, a tight feeling across her chest constraining her effort to breathe. She blinked again, harder, until her vision started to clear.

Kind of. She winced, trying to make sense of what she saw. She bit back a moan as the bones in her right leg started to knit back together. She was lying down in a dark, dank place, with bars on three sides of her, a stone wall behind her. That was about as much as she could see, as she waited for the swelling in her brain to disperse.

"Vassi? Are you okay?" Max's voice echoed through the darkness toward her, concern evident in his tone. Springs creaked, and she heard the light pad of feet on stone as he crossed to the bars separating them.

"Uh-huh," she groaned as her body's natural healing process kicked in. As a half-blood, it took a little longer to mend, but she would. She needed blood to heal quicker, and to take away some of this pain. She looked down at herself. She was strapped to some sort of bed.

"Why am I tied down?" she asked, hissing as her broken leg popped a shard of bone back into place.

"They didn't know how you would react when you woke," he said, and sighed. "God, you scared me. When I came to, I thought you were dead."

She chuckled, the sound dry and raspy in her throat. "Technically, I was, but it takes more than just a few broken bones and busted organs to keep a good vampire down, Max."

Another sigh. "Ryder."

The grey fog descended again, obscuring his words in her memory, and she winced. She knew it annoyed him. It annoyed everybody, but there wasn't anything she could do about it. Her mother had once told her that her abilities made her see the true essence of a person, and therefore a better suited name.

Screw her gift. She'd just like, for once, to have a normal conversation. She extended her talons, wincing when one didn't stretch with the others. Damn. Her healing abilities only extended as far as her original body. She'd have to go to a miscreant healer to fix that—if she got out of here.

"Where are we?" she asked as she contorted her wrist, slicing through the leather straps that bound her.

"I believe the Woodland Pack have caught us, after all."

She grimaced as she sat up. "They crossed boundaries to do it. Summercliff might border on the Woodland area, but the bulk of it is squarely in Nightwing territory." It was one of the reasons she'd selected the town. She swung her legs off the bed and stared at the floor for a moment, trying to assess their situation. It wasn't looking good.

"I thought Nightwing was safe?"

"So did I." Damn. "Either the wolves trespassed—and they'll catch hell for it if they did—or they were allowed access."

"Why would Nightwing give them access?"

She grimaced. "Because the Nightwing vampire prime doesn't like the Armstrong family."

"How do you know that?"

"That vampire prime is my client." Was, she thought moodily. She'd miscalculated Vivianne Marchetta's reaction at her defence of the son of her competitor. And if she hadn't, then she'd instigated one hell of mess for the vamp with her wolf neighbours.

Max shifted. Her eyes were getting better. She must have knocked her head in the accident, but she was slowly getting her night vision back. He'd bowed his head, his hands on the bars.

"Damn him," he said, so quiet she presumed he didn't want her to hear it.

"Damn who? Jared Gray? The Woodland lycan who caught us?"

Max shook his bowed head. "No, my father." He ran one hand through his dark hair, his profile strong and stark against the stone wall behind him. "I thought by walking away I could, well," he shrugged, "walk away. That I wouldn't have to live in his shadow anymore, or be associated with whatever crap he did." The muscles in his jaw flexed. "But it seems he's pissed off too many people for that."

"He's still your father, Max."

"And I'll never be able to forget it."

She rose from the bunk, putting her weight gingerly on her still-mending leg. His eagerness to shed family like a snakeskin, too tight and constrictive for his liking, infuriated her. "Maybe you shouldn't forget it. You have a family who will support you. Do you know how valuable that is?"

Max lifted his head to glare at her. "You don't understand."

"You're right, I don't understand," she hissed, her anger flaring to life like embers under new fuel. "I don't understand how you can turn your back and just walk away from the people who love you. You had a home, you had a life surrounded by people who share your interests—who share your *blood*, and who accept you for who you are. Do you realise how precious that is? Yet you discard it so easily, like used trash."

He blinked at her for a moment, and she tried to regain a glimmer of control to mask her anger, her pain … her envy.

"Sometimes it's better for everyone to just walk away."

She snorted. "That sounds like something a quitter would say."

Max's grip tightened on the rails, and she saw the white of bone beneath knuckles. "You don't know what you're talking about."

She nodded as she advanced toward the rails, her eyes glowing. She was fed up with dancing around lies and half-truths. "You are so right. I don't know you or your family." She tilted her head to the side. "And I don't know how you can poison a patient in your surgery and not call it murder. I don't know how a 'mostly' human can keep up with a vampire or a wolf at a full run, or how you could sneak into a wolf's den and not be caught, or how I didn't see you in the forest until you were on top of me—and believe me, I was on high alert." She stopped when her face was mere inches away from his, her hand reaching for a bar. She hissed at the burn and immediately let go, shaking off the sting. Silver. Damn it. She peered into the silver-blue gaze that was so mesmerising, so full of light, yet hiding so much. "And I don't know how you managed to throw lycan guardians off our scent. So yes, I don't know who or what you really are."

For all she knew, he was a stone-cold killer.

Max's chin jutted forward. "Well, I guess we all have our secrets." His voice was a low murmur as his gaze dropped to her mouth. "Why don't we make a deal—I'll tell you everything you want to know, if you tell me all about this kiss-and-tell trick of yours. Or why a vampire has talons."

Vassi's head jerked back, and Max nodded, his eyebrows lifting in curiosity.

"Oh, that's a bit of a sensitive spot, I see."

There was a grating noise, and the door beyond their cells swung open. A lycan carrying a lantern walked in, eyeing them carefully as more dark figures trooped in.

"Alpha Prime wants to talk with you."

* * *

Ryder caught Vassiliki as she was shoved from behind, and he stopped to face the lycan. "Back off," he said through clenched teeth. They needn't be so rough—not with Vassi. Him, fine, but Vassi—they were going to take care, damn it.

The lycan smiled. "Or what? You're not really in a position to make demands, human."

Ryder smiled back. Let them underestimate him. "Be careful with her."

The lycan tilted his head. "Aw, the dentist is sweet on his lawyer." The other lycan sniggered as they shoved both Ryder and Vassiliki into motion again.

Ryder pursed his lips. There were only three of them. He could take them, but possibly not before one of them harmed Vassi. And they were right, he was sweet on his lawyer, even if she was hiding something from him, didn't trust him, thought he was a killer and drove him crazy with her hot kisses and cold retreats.

He walked on, putting as much of his body between Vassi and the lycans as possible.

Woodland Pack's den must be beneath the mountains. Like the Alpine den, the caves and corridors seemed clean and uncluttered, but unlike the rocky flooring of the Alpine tunnels, in this den the ground they walked upon was dirt. Following Vassi through the snow had been easy, he could hide his tracks in hers. Here, though, they left tracks. He could veil, but he couldn't hide his tracks.

"I don't get it." Vassi said in a low voice beside him, his gut clenching as the sound reached in and tweaked at his libido. This was so not the time or place. The instinct to reach out and touch her, even if it was to give her comfort and protection, was hard to control.

"What?"

"Why are we still alive? If we were both out cold after the crash, they could have killed us easily enough then. Why bring us back here?"

She had a point, and all the scenarios he ran through his mind did not have positive outcomes.

"Perhaps they're still trying to figure out a few things," she said quietly.

Ryder shifted closer as he tried to catch her words.

"Like what?"

"Like why you would poison an alpha, for one," she muttered.

He frowned. It was the second time she'd said it. "You keep saying that." He did not kill Jared Gray. At least, not intentionally.

"The M.E.'s prelim report came back. Gray was killed by a dose of wolfsbane found in your putty."

Ryder halted, only to be shoved by a rough hand in the middle of his back. He shot a dark glare over his shoulder at the lycan guardian, before resuming his journey to wherever they hell they were going inside the bowels of this mountain. "I didn't put it there. Somebody set me up."

Wolfsbane was a toxin. Sometimes, in extremely mild doses, it could be used to treat some miscreant conditions, but he'd found other, less lethal remedies also did the trick, and preferred to use those that didn't have such a high mortality rate.

"Does anybody else work in your surgery?"

"No."

"No assistants?"

"No. It's a start-up. There's just me at the moment. It's hard to find assistants that can hold their own against a pain-crazed miscreant."

"Shut up and keep walking," that same lycan said from behind, and gave them both a push. Ryder saw Vassi's eyes flare briefly, before she banked her anger. She stepped closer, and Ryder leaned down to catch her next words.

"What about break-ins? Had any problems with people gaining access into your clinic?"

"No." If there was one thing he'd learned from his father, it was how to build exceptional security for his practice. He stored some drugs on the premises, drugs that some miscreants developed a craving for. Some humans did, too. Wolfsbane, though, was not one of them.

They walked out into a large cave, and Vassi paused for a moment at the number of figures gathered along the walls of the reception hall. The lycan reached out to push her again, but Ryder was faster, grasping the wrist of the lycan with a warning look.

"Don't."

The lycan bared his teeth. Ryder shot him an exasperated look. "I'm a dentist. Teeth don't scare me." He grinned, showing his own. "I'm going to enjoy pulling yours out."

"Relax, Winston. Let our guests come forward."

Ryder turned to the source of the voice. The lycan lolled indolently in his chair, smiling benignly down at them from the raised platform upon which he sat. With dark, shaggy hair and a close-cropped beard, the man already looked part wolf in his human form.

"Who are you?" Ryder asked calmly. He could hazard a guess, but he didn't want to give the alpha the satisfaction of observing his rank.

"I'm Rafe, Alpha Prime of Woodland Pack." The lycan made a rolling gesture with his hand that Ryder presumed was meant to be courtly. The lycans gathered around the walls of the cave watched silently, tension so thick in the air it was almost suffocating.

Vassi cocked her head to the side. "You seem more of a Hugo. What do you want?"

Ryder almost smiled in satisfaction when the alpha prime blinked in surprise at her comment. It was nice to know he wasn't the only one she renamed—although renaming alpha primes wasn't necessarily a good survival tactic.

Rafe frowned slightly, assessing the lawyer before deciding to ignore her comment and answer her question. He gave a slow smile, his teeth bared. Ryder stiffened. Even from here, he could see the lycan's teeth had been enhanced. The work would have been expensive, his fangs longer, sharper than natural.

"Ah, that is the question, isn't it? What do I want?" The dark-haired man crossed his ankle over his knee. His pose was casual, but Ryder could see the sharp interest in the man's gaze. Casual, perhaps. Dangerous, definitely.

"I have caught the Alpha Killer," the alpha prime continued, "and I'm in a unique position where I can get anything I want."

Ryder adjusted his stance, setting his feet apart as he folded his arms. "Which is?"

"Hmm, I haven't decided yet."

"He's lying," Vassi whispered. Ryder glanced at her. She was focused on the lycan, her expression a mask of cool indifference, but her eyes—they weren't the dark chocolate-brown of her normal state, nor the golden or red glow when she got riled or ready to attack. No, now her eyes were black, a dark miasma of secrets and power he was just beginning to suspect she held within her.

She was giving nothing away, though, and it seemed no one had heard her but him.

Ryder turned back to the lycan. "Why are we here?" He kept his tone patient. This lycan was different to Jared's mate, Samantha. He seemed laidback, but there was threat inherent in his pose, in his gaze ... in his smile.

"You killed an alpha prime, Galen. You're public enemy number one among all shifter tribes. Even the bears are hunting you, which is saying something."

Ryder frowned. "I understand Woodland is in conflict with Alpine—"

"Woodland is in conflict with pretty much everyone," Vassi muttered, and Rafe laughed at her comment.

"You have it right, counsellor. We are living in a fractious time. Woodland needs to protect its borders." The lycan beckoned at one of the females standing off to the side, and she threw him an apple. He caught it, gazed at it for a moment, before slowly sinking his teeth into it.

Ryder again stared at the fangs. They'd lengthened, almost with a vampiric quality, yet Rafe still retained his human form. He idly wondered how the teeth would look if the lycan shifted into his beast.

Rafe chewed for a moment, then swallowed. "I want to extend into Alpine territory, and I now have something Alpine wants." His smile was more a flashing of those intriguing teeth. "I think we can work out a trade."

Ryder kept his expression remote. From what he'd heard of Woodland in the past, they rarely negotiated.

Rafe shrugged. "Or I could simply kill you for daring to murder an alpha prime, and nobody could touch me."

"I'm an officer of the court, Hugo. You can't enforce tribal law here, the court has already ruled. You must observe the legal protection both I and my client deserve, otherwise there are consequences."

Ryder frowned. Vassi's tone had been calm, but the words would be seen as a challenge to any alpha.

Rafe's smile broadened, although it still didn't quite reach his eyes. "Ms. Verity, you are in my territory now. Your court has no jurisdiction here."

"Speaking of jurisdiction, you entered Nightwing territory to find us. Just curious—did you have permission?"

Rafe eyed her for a moment. "Of course. You underestimate how much we werefolks want to see your client pay for his crime."

Ryder could see Vassi's shoulders lower as her tension relaxed.

"Liar," she breathed quietly, not moving her lips as she kept her gaze on the alpha prime.

Ryder didn't give any sign of having heard her, although his brain was racing. If what Vassi stated was true, the lycan had broken tribal law by trespassing into vampire territory. That was quite a risk, antagonising a neighbouring colony.

"You seem very invested, Hugo. Someone would think perhaps too invested, as though you may have had something to do with Jared Gray's murder ..." Vassi wasn't asking a question, Ryder noticed. Her tone was soft and accusing, as though she was deliberately trying to provoke the alpha.

Rafe stilled, his eyes narrowing as he stared at the vampire. The lycan rose from his seat. "You insult me, half-blood." He stepped down off the platform. "To kill an alpha outside of tribal warfare is a crime. You're accusing *me* of murder?"

"You only seem to follow the rules when it suits you," Vassi commented innocently, and Ryder frowned. The lycan was getting angry, and she was purposely aggravating him. But she wasn't finished. She too, folded her arms, her stance mimicking Ryder's own relaxed pose. "It seems to me, Hugo, that if you have a beef with Alpine over territory, the alpha prime's death would be of benefit to you."

Rafe rumbled for a moment, low in his throat. "A coincidence—and stop calling me Hugo."

Vassi shook her head. "I don't think so, Hugo. Did you have anything to do with Jared Gray's death?"

The alpha growled as he sprang at Vassi. Ryder reacted, putting himself between the alpha prime and the lawyer. The lycan landed a hair's breadth from his feet. The wolf glared into Ryder's eyes as the guardians dragged him back before shifting his gaze to Vassiliki, his face close to hers as he seethed at her question. "I. Did. Not."

Ryder tried unsuccessfully to shake off the two guardians as they clamped their fists on his arms, holding him still. He stiffened, his eyes on the alpha prime, and the vamp standing her ground.

"Ease up, Rafe." A female detached from the crowd, her tall, athletic frame moving with a smooth grace, an impassive look on her face. "There is still the question of a trial."

Rafe turned to glare at the she-wolf, and Ryder realised the woman had earned the ire of her alpha prime with her remark. The alpha lowered his head in a nod of acknowledgment, but Ryder felt it was more of a warning than an agreement. Rafe then chuckled, his breath stirring Vassi's dark locks. "You are an interesting creature, Ms. Verity." He raised his head, his gaze switching to Ryder. "But I don't wish to waste any more time. You'll be handed over to the Alpine Pack for judgment. Ms. Verity will be given safe passage through Woodland territory."

A muscle clenched in Ryder's jaw. Damn it. If he was handed over to the Alpine Pack he'd be killed within minutes, and any hope of finding out what had really happened to Jared Gray, or of clearing his name, would die with him.

Vassi turned to gaze at him, her eyes still that disturbing black, her mouth tight. "You were right, after all."

"About what?" he asked as she was hauled off down another tunnel.

"About everything," she called back over her shoulder, and then she was gone, shoved around the bend of the tunnel, out of his sight.

Ryder frowned. Everything? He'd told her he hadn't murdered Jared Gray, that someone was setting him up.

He gazed at the alpha prime who now studied him, his hands on his hips, eyes narrowed. If Rafe had tried to kill Jared Gray directly, it would have sparked a war between the packs, one that would sorely test the Woodland alpha prime's capability of also fighting his disputes with other tribes. But if someone else killed the alpha for him, and he then presented that killer to the Alpine Pack, he could request land be given as a boon.

Could the Woodland alpha be that Machiavellian?

"Escort him back to the cells. I'll have to set up a meeting with Samantha Alpine." Rafe gave Ryder a little smile, then turned to stride back up to his chair, beckoning over the lone female who'd dared question him in front of his pack.

Ryder was dragged around, but a movement caught his eye. One of the lycans on the edge of the hall had moved, his head down as he skirted behind another. Ryder's eyes narrowed as he followed the figure, ignoring the shoves that tried to push him back in the direction of the tunnel that led to the cells.

There was something about that lycan, something that teased at a memory, niggling at him with the annoying persistence of the sting of a mosquito. The lycan passed beneath a torch, the flame's light sputtering over his features, and Ryder halted.

"Wait," he called out.

The lycan turned, and the guardians pulling Ryder toward the tunnel stopped.

"You—I know you." Where the hell had he seen the lycan? Everyone stilled in the room, the gathered lycans holding their breath. Ryder didn't check, but he heard the conversation between Rafe and the female lycan halt, felt the weight of the alpha prime's stare upon him.

The lycan dipped his head again, and the movement dragged the memory into his mind's eye. He'd ducked his head exactly that way as he'd presented the delivery docket for Ryder to sign.

"You're the courier," Ryder breathed, and everything started to slide into place. The lycan had delivered his latest supply order a week ago, had even helped him carry the goods into his clinic. Including the tainted pot that had poisoned Jared Gray.

"It was you," Ryder said, his voice strong. He turned to Rafe on his pretentious little platform. "You killed Jared Gray."

The alpha prime bared his teeth, and a collective growl rose from the gathered lycans. Rafe rose from his seat, shifting into wolf form as he did so. The rest of the lycans in the hall did the same, and suddenly Ryder found himself surrounded by wolves, slowly advancing toward him.

Chapter Nine

Vassi noticed the change in light as the tunnel angled upwards. The silvery glow from the moon was bright enough for her to notice the determined expression on her guards' faces. They were getting close to the exit. She didn't have much time.

"So, are you just going to let me wander the forest on my own, or take me to the nearest town?"

"We'll take you to the boundary," the lycan answered her, his grip tightening on her arm. A cold chill washed over her, and she hid her shudder by jerking on her arm. The lycan didn't let go.

He and his partner had no intention of releasing her at the boundary.

She'd met some good liars in her time, but the Woodland alpha prime was easily one of the best. He'd stared right into her eyes and told her he'd had nothing to do with Jared Gray's death, all the while his deceit had chilled her to the bone.

The Woodland Pack had no intention of delivering Max to the Alpine she-wolf. She could only assume that the alpha prime was going to kill him. She tried to free her arm again, and the lycan growled at her as he pulled her up the tunnel's incline to push past the foliage masking the entrance. His companion was close on her heels. She couldn't understand the end game, though. The Woodland alpha could ask for a boon from Alpine for delivering their alpha's killer. Or would he claim that Max had tried to escape, resulting in his death?

But why kill her, too? She was an officer of the court. She wasn't overly arrogant in believing that her death during the investigation of a case would result in a major media storm and punitive action against the Woodland Pack. Every court officer worked under a global protection, and while the court allowed for tribal jurisdiction and practices, they would enforce that law of protection to the maximum penalty—with the support of all other tribes. That was the basis of Reformation—tribes could have their own jurisdictions, but all miscreants and humans were subject to Reformed Law—in an effort to keep all creatures on a level playing field.

While Woodland Pack was rebellious and openly hostile to neighbouring tribes, she couldn't see them taking on Reform as well. She didn't have all the pieces to the puzzle, and if she let these lycans do what they planned, she never would.

She summoned her gift as she trudged between the two lycans, the crunch of pine needles under their boots and their breathing the only sound in that section of the woods.

"So, you're going to let me go, aren't you?" She needed to make sure.

"Yes, you'll be free when we get to the border," the lycan on her left responded dryly.

Cold. It blanketed her, revealing their lethal intent. She nodded. "Just what I thought."

Her fangs stretched, as did her talons. She winced at the one injured talon that scraped the inside of her finger in a futile attempt to push through, but she didn't have time to inspect it. She slashed her arms out either side of her body, catching each lycan across their stomach and around their side. Both of them howled, shifting immediately into wolf form as they whirled to attack.

Vassi was ready for them, bending low on one knee, her other leg stretching out as she whipped her arms out. The lycan who'd been closer to her, the one who had answered her, yelped as she sliced through his pelt. She ducked as his companion jumped at her. His teeth snapped, but she jerked her neck out of reach, curling her fingers and striking up. Her talons pierced his lower jaw, sliding up through the mouth cavity to stab through the top of his snout.

She quickly withdrew her weapons from his jaw, using her index talon to slice him open from neck to navel.

The metallic scent of blood exploded, like a dark silk spreading across the earth, fogging her brain with the need to spill and drink blood. Her body craved it, starved from the self-healing she'd endured. She turned back to the first lycan just as he sprang at her. She raised her forearm, catching him under his jaw and, exposing his neck, she pounced, bearing him back onto the ground as her fangs sank into his throat.

It was over in a matter of minutes, the wolves' bodies lying at broken angles, their blood staining the ground beneath them. Vassi wiped her lips. She'd drunk as much as she needed to satisfy the hunger that rose at the scent of the ruby liquid, and she could feel it surging through her system, strengthening her, completing her healing.

She should run. She should race down to the Woodland boundary, cross into Nightwing territory and contact Reform Court for assistance. But by the time anyone got here, Max would be dead.

She couldn't let that happen. She turned and ran back to the tunnel, a dark hole in a dark forest, arms up as she crashed through the foliage at the entrance, her eyes adjusting to the dimming light as she sped toward her human.

She was rounding a bend in the corridor when she felt it—a warm wind that billowed up the tunnel, followed by a blinding flash of light, and a shock wave that lifted her off her feet and slammed her into the stone wall.

× × ×

Ryder ran through the tunnel, the unconscious lycan courier over his shoulder. His explosion had knocked out everyone in the reception hall, but the effects would only last for a few minutes. Soon he'd have all of Woodland Pack on his tail. He

rounded a bend and almost tripped over Vassi's legs. She was
dazed, her eyes wide as she stared around her. There were
piles of rock that scattered along the corridor, and he
grimaced. He hadn't known she was anywhere near, hadn't
intended to hurt her with his latest power surge.

He reached down and grasped her arm, dragging her to
her feet. "We need to move," he said.

She still looked confused, gazing about in shock at the
corridor, then at the lycan over his shoulder.

"What—?"

He bent low to make eye contact with her. "Vassi, we
need to move. Now."

She blinked, and her confusion cleared as she nodded.
They ran, bursting out into the moonlit forest. He panted as
they darted between trees. He narrowly avoided tripping over
the corpses of two werewolves. It didn't take a witch to divine
what had happened there. If they weren't already dead, he
would have killed them himself for trying to hurt Vassi. He
threw the teeth he'd ripped from Winston on his way out,
casting them like pebbles over the two corpses. Let that be a
warning to them.

He continued to run, purposely avoiding the trail, wanting
to make any pursuit as difficult as possible through the
undergrowth. He stumbled, caught hold of a tree limb to
regain his balance, then ran after the vamp. He'd expended a
lot of energy with that blast, and the lycan over his shoulder
was a deadweight.

"Over here," Vassi called over her shoulder as she
switched direction. They bolted out onto a service track, and
he smiled when he saw the fleet of black SUVs parked in a
clearing. He opened the rear of the nearest vehicle and
dropped the lycan unceremoniously into the space, his smile
broadening at the thunk he heard as the lycan's head hit
something hard.

Vassi climbed into the driver's seat, so he ran around to
the side, jumping into the vehicle as Vassi turned the engine

over and slid it into gear. Tyres skidded on gravel and bark until they found traction, then the car surged forward.

"Who's your friend?" Vassi asked over the roar of the engine as she sped along the service road.

Ryder turned from the window. As yet, he couldn't see any wolves in pursuit, but they didn't have much of a head start. He surveyed the woman who was glaring out at the road with a stern expression. She looked angry.

"He's a witness," he told her, sliding his butt across the seat so that he could brace himself against the dashboard as she drove at a reckless pace down the mountain. "He delivered my last order of supplies to the clinic." He blinked slowly. He'd expended a great deal of energy over the last couple of days, and using enough lightforce to create a blast big enough to knock out a whole den of werewolves had left him feeling lethargic.

"You think he knows something about the wolfsbane?" The car swerved as she took the turn onto the highway at high speed, shifting down in gear with the ease of a NASCAR rally driver.

"Yes," he said soberly, and he rested his head against his seat. "But whether I can get him to talk in court is another thing entirely."

She nodded, her eyes on the road. "Trust me, he'll talk."

Ryder eyed her speculatively. She drove with a single-minded focus, her reflexes lightning fast as they sped through the night. Lights flashed, slowly illuminating her face. Her alabaster skin was smooth in its perfection, an interesting contrast of concealment and revealment as the road lights bathed them from darkness to full light, then darkness again. Her lips were pulled in a firm line, her brow furrowed. Her hair was a mass of midnight, her lips a pouty bow of scarlet. He'd known her for such a short time but was finding it easier to read her, to gauge her emotions—and yet she was becoming even more of a mystery. Right now, she was keeping her anger under tight control.

He'd worked with enough vampires to know that a fresh kill and a rush of adrenalin were ingredients for an all-out blood craze, and she'd just survived an encounter with two werewolves. Even though she was only a half-blood, she still had to be battling some pretty harsh instincts to rip something—or someone—to shreds.

He frowned. She'd nearly died—all because she'd landed his case, a random act that was having unforeseen ripple effects through her life. Earlier, she couldn't go to her home for fear of a lycan attack. Now, having survived an attempted murder-across-kind, the Woodland Pack would be on her trail just as much as his. If word got out about what had happened, or nearly happened, then Woodland would be facing critical punishment and embargoes from all other tribes. And then there was the Nightwing issue. He sighed. Hell. This thing was snowballing so far and so fast beyond his control. Where had he miscalculated? Triggering the Reform Law over tribal jurisdiction by handing himself in should have avoided this mess of complicated crap. And now he'd dragged Vassi right into the middle of it.

"I'm sorry," he said softly, his gaze on her face. She flicked him a quick glance, surprise and confusion evident before she turned her attention back to the road.

"You have nothing to be sorry for," she told him, then shrugged. "I know you didn't kill Jared Gray. You were used. Like a weapon."

He frowned. He didn't like that deduction. It implied a lack of control, of foresight … a weakness, to be wielded by someone else's hand, for a purpose not his own. He was a light warrior, and light warriors were masters of their fate, not somebody else's bitch.

"Don't worry, Max. We'll get to the bottom of it." She looked at him again, her expression resolute. "Woodland will pay."

His frown deepened. "That sounds like a threat." He closed his eyes as realisation struck. "Damn it, you can't use this as an excuse for tribal warfare."

There was a long-running feud between the vampires and werewolves, one that flared up at the least provocation. Lycans trying to kill a half-blood court officer would be enough justification to launch another episode of tribal warfare.

Vassi's lips twisted. "Relax, Max. There will be no tribal warfare."

His eyes narrowed. There was something in her tone, something that made him ignore the brief flare of annoyance at her use of that nickname for him. Instead, it was the interesting combination of little-girl-lost and bitter determination that caught his attention. Her family would be within its rights to exercise some form of retribution—did she plan on taking on the Woodland Pack herself?

She noticed his confusion, his wariness, and sighed. "Tribal warfare needs family, then tribal support. I have neither."

"You have no family?"

She laughed, although there was something so sad about the breathy sound. "None that would care."

He eyed her for a long moment, but she kept her gaze on the road. He'd go to war for her. The thought came out of nowhere, surprising him. He hadn't felt anything like that, not since ... well, not for a long time.

He shifted in his seat to gaze directly out the windscreen. He hadn't realised. He got the impression her lack of family wasn't through choice, not like his. Still, it was something they had in common.

The next ridge was backlit, its rocky outline visible against the night sky. Irondell lay beyond that ridge, the city's lights giving an eerie glow to the landscape. She was one vampire— a half-blood at that, waging a little war on his behalf against the werewolf tribes of the east coast.

"I'm going to hire an attorney," he said abruptly, keeping his gaze on the white road markings that passed under them at a hypnotic pace.

"What? Why?" He saw her dark hair fall over her shoulder as she whipped around to stare at him, dividing her focus between him and the road.

He shrugged. "You were right. I have the money, after all, and I'll need a damn good defence against the Woodland Pack."

The interior of the car was quiet, just the humming of tyres on asphalt interrupting the silence, along with the sound of the lycan's breathing behind them.

"I believe you, Max. You didn't commit murder. I can help you."

Ryder smiled, although it felt more of a grimace. "You said yourself, you don't need to believe me to do your job. I'm sure that goes for most lawyers."

"True—but you'll stand a better chance with me on your side."

"No. Thank you for the offer, but once we get to town I think we should separate. You can go to Reform Court and file whatever paperwork is required to release you from my case."

They crested the ridge and looked down on the city below, all lit up. Ryder couldn't help but think how a dark and dangerous place such as Irondell could look so achingly beautiful, nestled in the arms of darkest night.

"Why won't you accept my help?" Vassi's tone showed her perplexity.

He pursed his lips. She wasn't going to let it go. He was pretty sure that any other lawyer would be burning rubber to get to the courthouse and relinquish legal rights to his case. But not Vassi—why? Did she have an inflated sense of justice? Or a deflated sense of self-preservation? Either way, he had to get her off his case—if only to protect the stubborn, sexy vamp lawyer. But he had to make her want to drop his case.

"I think I can do better," he told her, turning to gaze at her. "So far you've taken me on some wild-goose chase into the wilds, I've nearly been killed by werewolves, and I have no real clear defence planned for a trial that starts on Monday. Drop me off downtown." He kept his tone calm, his expression remote, and winced on the inside at the cruelty of his words.

Her eyes darkened, taking on the obsidian secrets she wouldn't share with him. "Actually, we know Jared Gray was loved and respected by his pack, that Woodland Pack would do anything to extend their territory into the Alpine region, including pissing off their neighbouring vampire colony, and that the lycan you stole may have even more information. I'd say that's a pretty good effort, so far." She smiled as she turned off the highway and took a ramp directly into the red light district. "So you see, Max, you'll need to do better than that if you want to get rid of me."

"Fine. You want to hear it? I'd like a lawyer who can at least get my name right, one that's not going to get me killed because she's only a half-blood and not strong enough to go up against full-blooded werewolves on a blood hunt." He shrugged, even though she was staring at him with those beautiful, dark, mesmerising eyes of hers. "I need more than you're capable of delivering, Vassi. That's why I want to let you go and find someone else to do this job."

Clothing rustled in the back, then the lycan sat up, his eyes glowing as he bared his teeth in a dangerous growl. In the blink of an eye, he launched himself at the back of Vassi's head.

Ryder reacted instantly, channelling his lightforce into a single blow to the head that knocked the lycan out cold before his jaws could snap at Vassi's pretty little neck.

"My case in point," he muttered. Vassi glanced over her shoulder, her eyes wide. She hadn't had time to move, to defend herself. The lycan slumped back against the door, his head making a cracking sound as she drove around a corner. "I'm spending half my time looking out for you when I should be looking out for myself."

Her lips pursed, then her eyes narrowed. She was gazing at him as though she was trying to see inside his skull, inside his mind. A light dawned in her eyes, as though she'd just realised something, but her expression gave nothing else away.

"Where will you go, Max? Who is going to help you? Because you'll need it. This lycan isn't just going to sit down over a hot cup of camomile tea and share stories with you."

Ryder shrugged. "I'll manage."

She slowed down, turning the car with care down a narrow alley. He frowned. "Where are we?"

"I know someone who can help us with your lycan, Max. If you'll trust me." She braked, pulling the car to a stop as a roller door slid open with a rough rattle.

A man stood in the doorway, one hand holding the door open, the other holding the collar of an unconscious man. Muted light filtered out from the garage, but it was all behind the tall, bulky figure, casting his features in shadow. Ryder could make out jeans, boots and a bare chest, and what looked like a pair of sunglasses, although why the man would be wearing them at this time of night he had no idea. The tall figure strode forward and carelessly tossed the unconscious man out into the alley. He turned to face their car, his face still in the shadows, but Ryder noticed the dark markings of a tattoo on his bicep. The man looked dangerous. Lethal.

Ryder arched an eyebrow and glanced at Vassiliki.

She smiled. "Trust me."

Chapter Ten

Vassi's smile broadened as she approached the tall figure in the garage. "Hey, Dave."

She sensed Max slowly getting out of the car, and flicked him a glance. His expression was remote as he folded his arms. The movement added bulk to his impressive physique as he sized up her friend. He looked so dark and sexy and forbidding. Since they'd been abducted by the Woodland Pack Max had changed, showing a darker side to his personality, a lethal determination that was intriguing. His nerd factor was on the wane. She switched her gaze back to her former client in an effort to ignore the allure of her companion.

Dave nodded. "Vassi." His voice was deep, his tone warm. She stared at him for a moment, trying to gauge his reaction to her visit, and then the big guy finally smiled and held out his arms. "It's been a while."

She hugged him, grinning. "Yes it has. How have you been?"

Dave shrugged. "Same old, same old, darlin'." He slung an arm over her shoulder, tugging her to his side as he faced her companion. "And who is this?"

"This is my client, Max," she responded.

"Ryder," he corrected as he held out his hand. "Ryder Galen."

"Whatever." She turned to her friend, noticing that for once the mental fog over her client's words wasn't as thick or heavy. "We need your help."

Dave arched an eyebrow. "Let me guess, you're finally going to let me ink you up."

She laughed. "No." She turned to Max. "Dave is a tattooist."

"I prefer the term tattoo artist. I create art, Vassi darlin'."

"He's also a witch," she told Max, and smiled when his dark eyebrows rose. He gave her a considering look before turning back to the sunglass-wearing hulk next to her.

"Pleased to meet you," Dave said, extending his hand in greeting.

Max eyed it warily before clasping it.

She felt Dave stiffen next to her. "Well, well, what do we have here," Dave murmured. Vassi eyed her friend with surprise as he continued to hold on to Max's hand.

"You're quite the surprise, aren't you?"

Max's eyes narrowed. "So are you."

Vassi frowned. "Uh, okay, well, why don't we talk about surprises inside Dave's shop instead of outside in this alley where any werewolf can join in?" She had no idea what they were talking about, but now wasn't the time to start a bromance.

Dave frowned back at her. "Are you bringing trouble to my business, Vassi?"

She snorted. "Your business *is* trouble, Dave. We have a lycan in the back who needs a little friendly encouragement to chat. I was hoping you could help."

Max went to the rear of the car and opened it. In a moment, he'd hauled out the unconscious lycan and hefted him over his shoulder in a fireman's lift. He turned to look at the unconscious body that Dave had tossed into the alley. "What's with him?"

"Apparently he didn't like what I did with his girlfriend. Of course, I disagreed." Dave smiled as he stood aside, extending his arm toward his garage. "Please, come in."

Vassi gestured for Max to precede her, and jumped up to grab the base of the roller door and pulled it down. She walked behind him, watching his hips swing with a lazy sensuality that made her want to reach out and stroke him.

She smiled. He'd tried to fire her. Warmth spread through her at the memory. Those things he'd said to her in the car, those words which should have been cruel, should have been like glass splinters scraping at her core, those words he'd uttered to get her to leave … they were all lies.

She'd felt the bitter coldness of his deceit, and it had taken her a moment to figure out what he was doing.

Her client was trying to protect her.

She'd been more surprised by that fact than the words she'd known he'd carefully chosen for maximum impact.

Dave led them down a short hall to a door. He opened the door, revealing a flight of stairs leading down, lit by a couple of fluorescent bulbs. He gestured for Max to precede him. Vassi followed, but had to stop at the threshold as an unrelenting invisible force held her back. She raised an eyebrow at her friend.

"Would you like to invite me in, Dave?" she asked him sweetly.

Dave smiled, the expression friendly. "By all means, Vassi, you are welcome as my guest." He emphasised the last word.

She nodded, appreciating his trust, and the inherent warning in his words. He wasn't being rude, just cautious. Not many witches allowed vampires into their havens. As a guest, she had to abide by strict rules, or else access could be revoked.

She strode downstairs, giving enough space for Max to precede her so she didn't come in contact with the lycan slung over his shoulders. If what Max said was true, then this lycan could possibly tell them who was behind Jared's murder, and why. Well, frankly, she didn't care that much, as long as she got enough information to cast doubt on her client's motives.

And then she'd take on Woodland Pack. She couldn't help it. Something innate was triggered within a vampire at the hands of a werewolf—and vice versa. An intuitive vendetta between the two tribes that flared constantly throughout the ages. There was even a clause in the Reform Law to recognise it and award special dispensation. She couldn't let what they'd tried to do to her slide. It set a bad example. No, she would have to exact some retribution against them, not only on behalf of vampires, but also for all the court officers she represented. No pack could get away with what Woodland had attempted to do. Of course, if she'd had family that gave a damn, things would be easier. She'd been honest when she'd told Max there would be no tribal warfare. She didn't have a tribe invested in protecting her interests, or her. She'd have to do it on her own.

Another door at the bottom of the stairs requiring yet another invitation from the resident, security-conscious witch, and then they were in a series of caves beneath Dave's tattoo parlour.

"What is this place?" Max breathed as he halted, staring about in awe.

They'd stepped into a large cavern, and Dave carelessly waved a hand, bringing what looked like several hundred candles to life.

"This, my curious friend, is Old Irondell." Dave turned, the markings on his skin clearly visible in the candlelight. The tattoos were all over his back, not images but text in a gothic script that rolled over his muscles, up over his shoulders and down his arms. Darkly beautiful. Vassi had always wondered about the dark markings but had never worked up the courage to ask. "You can put your little friend in there," Dave said, pointing to a cell.

Dave had used the natural rock formations to form smaller rooms around the rim of the larger cave. There were more tunnels leading off in different directions, one dark hole revealing another tunnel leading further into the underground.

"Old Irondell? I thought that was only a legend," Max breathed, eyeing the dark hole at the end of the cave.

Dave snorted. "It's a legend to those who don't need to know." He pointed to Max "You don't need to know, so don't let on that you do."

Max dumped the lycan on the floor, and each of them ignored the man's groan.

Vassi joined Max and wandered through the cavern. Dave had set himself up a haven, a place to work his spells—and to take care of other witch business that Vassi didn't want to know about. She could understand Max's surprise. Old Irondell was part of the fable of Origin, before the Reformation, when changelings and witches and other miscreants had to hide their existence from the humans. Origin ended, though, when the miscreants revealed their existence, and then The Troubles began, resulting in a horrific war that saw deaths on all sides reach cataclysmic proportions and the destruction of many cities, including Old Irondell, before the Resolution that led to Reformation. The tunnels that ran under Irondell were the footprint of the city that once stood there—before it was burned to the ground, before the Reformation. From long, winding corridors to wide roads and plazas, it was a hidden metropolis. It was home to pockets of humanity and miscreants alike, and while everyone would like to believe Reform Law covered all, many knew there were some places that Reform Law couldn't touch. The less folks knew about Old Irondell, the safer they were.

Dave leaned against a scarred wooden table and folded his arms, his biceps bulging. "So, Vassi, what do you want me to do?"

"I want you to get this lycan to talk," she answered as Max approached her side.

"You don't need my help for that," Dave said, and she could feel his intent gaze, despite the barrier of the sunglasses he constantly wore.

She grimaced. "Actually, I do." Now that Max had taken her lipstick, she had no other way to compel the werewolf to tell her the truth.

"Well, perhaps you should be visiting your mother instead of me," Dave suggested.

Vassi's eyes widened. Dave knew. She swallowed. "When?" When did he find out? How did he find out?

Dave smiled dryly. "Always."

Her eyes narrowed. "You never said anything."

Dave shrugged. "I figured if you wanted me to know, you'd tell me."

"Tell you what?" Max asked, watching their exchange with a keen curiosity.

"Nothing," Vassi said abruptly. She folded her arms, mimicking Dave's stance. "Can you help me or not?" Damn witches saw way too much, sometimes.

Dave cocked his head to the side, his gaze flicking between the two. "Interesting." He bowed his head, as though thinking on something—or meditating, or whatever the hell witches did to make their friends squirm. He lifted his head to look at her.

"You know the rules. No innocents are harmed, and we do everything my way."

She nodded in relief. "Yep. No innocents."

"What do I get in exchange?"

Vassi frowned. "Can't you do a favour for a friend?"

Dave snorted. "If I had a dollar for every time someone said that to me ..."

Max shifted. "What do you want?"

Dave straightened from his casual pose, and Vassi became very aware of the strength and bulk of the man. He may not have the strength or speed of a shapeshifter, but he was a potent witch, and a powerful human. She considered him a special kind of friend, but she knew that witches had their own code. They were strong allies—unless you pissed them off. Then they became your worst nightmare. But not Dave. Not to her.

"I want a favour." Dave walked slowly forward.

Vassi nodded. "Oookay." Wasn't that what she'd asked? "What favour?"

Dave smiled. "I don't know yet. I want to bank it, use it when I need it."

For anyone else, Vassi would have refused, but this was Dave. She'd helped him out with some court issues and he'd helped her out in the past with some meditative training. They had shared a lot, and had been there when the other needed it. "Okay."

Dave shook his head. "But not from you, Vassi." He stood in front of Max. "I want it from you."

Max met his gaze squarely, his eyes narrowed as he assessed the tattoo artist. He flicked a glance to the unconscious lycan, then at Vassi, then back to the witch. Vassi held her breath. It was like watching two gladiators of old facing off.

Max finally nodded. "Fine. You have your favour."

He stuck his hand out, and Dave shook it, inclining his head. "One day, my friend."

Dave stepped back, then rubbed his hands together. "Right. Let's get started then. How do you want to do this, Vassi? Easy or hard?"

Vassi sighed. "Well, after what his pack tried to do, I'd like to go hard, but I still want him to talk, so maybe not *that* hard."

Dave nodded. "I see."

He stalked over to the cell and stepped inside to chain the lycan up. The man jerked, his eyes opening as the cuffs were clasped around his wrists and ankles. From where she stood, Vassi could hear the hiss as the metal burned against skin. She winced. The chains were painted with wolfsbane.

The lycan growled, trying to jerk his limbs free, only to cause himself more pain when his wrists and ankles came into contact with the corrosive poison.

Dave pulled a glass vial half-filled with a cloudy liquid out of his pocket, snapped off the lid and grasped the man's jaw.

He poured the fluid into the lycan's mouth, then stepped back as the lycan thrashed and tried to spit out the concoction, his growls turning to whimpers.

"Is this necessary?" Max stepped forward and Vassi placed her hand on his arm.

Dave nodded as he kept his eyes on the man on the floor. "A dilution of wolfsbane with a mild sedative. It'll weaken him so that he can't shift." He glanced over his shoulder. "I don't talk werewolf."

The witch strode out of the cell and across to a cupboard built along a wall, waving his hands with a flourish. The doors opened, revealing a massive array of bottles, boxes and books.

He removed a bottle of what looked like ash, and a number of other ingredients: powders, a bottle of liquid, some herbs and a silver dagger. He frowned. "Something's missing." He snapped his fingers and smiled. "Of course."

He strode over to a stereo built into a niche in the rock wall and switched it on. Thumping hard rock music echoed throughout the cavern and Dave nodded to the beat as he started to mix his potion. Every now and then his hips would sway to the music, or he'd step out to the beat, but nothing shook his focus as he worked quietly at the table.

Vassi watched in silence. Dave's lips moved quietly as he chanted something that sounded like garbled nonsense to her, but from the way the candles surrounding them stuttered and sparked it was obviously some powerful incantation.

She flicked a look at Max. His gaze was intent as he followed Dave's actions for a moment, then he raised his eyes to look at her. Just like that, the steady silver-blue stare met hers with a focus that left her breathless and made her think of all things dark and forbidden. He tilted his head as he stepped closer.

"So, Vassi, how do you know Dave?" His voice was low, and the witch was oblivious as he bopped along to the loud rock music.

She blinked, trying to stave off the familiar rise of attraction. "Uh, he's a friend. I represented him in a case against some vampires a couple of years ago, and since then we've stayed in touch."

He arched an eyebrow. "Is that all?" He leaned closer.

She nodded, then licked her lips nervously. She felt like she was being stalked by a shifter, one of those big, lazy cat breeds, with teeth. "Y-yes." She smiled. "I'm a vampire. He's a witch. All we can be is friends." Actually, they were more than friends, but not in the way Max was thinking. She'd helped Dave in a difficult time, and over the years Dave had helped her when her family wouldn't. That made him as good as family, in her eyes, and she'd do anything for him, as he would for her.

"Why? You don't think cross-breed relationships can work?"

She thought of her parents. While they'd loved each other, they hadn't loved enough to leave their families for the other, or to set up their own nucleus. Even a child wasn't enough motivation to forge a new life together. "No, I don't think they do. It's very challenging to cross conventions and create your own tribe."

His eyes narrowed. "That's a shame," he murmured softly. "Imagine what you could be missing out on."

"Right, you two, save your whispers for another time. I've got a client coming in for some outlining, so let's get this show on the road." Dave strode over to the cell, chalice in one hand, silver dagger in the other.

Chapter Eleven

Ryder watched as the tattoo artist trailed the blade across the lycan's forearm. Steam rose from the bloody mark left by the blade, and the skin started to blister. They'd chained the man to a wooden chair inside the cell for the purposes of their 'chat', but the lycan was proving remarkably stubborn.

"Did you know the supplies were tainted?" Dave asked calmly as the lycan writhed in pain.

"Go to hell," the lycan spat as sweat beaded his brow.

Dave tsked. "No, that place is reserved for you shifters." He casually dipped the dagger into the chalice, using it to stir the liquid before pulling it out. The liquid dripped onto the jean-clad leg of the lycan, and the man's chin rose as he tried to silence his cry of pain.

"I'm going to ask you again. Did you know the supplies were tainted?" Dave thrust the blade into the man's thigh. The lycan jolted, screaming in pain as the poison burnt through material and skin to the flesh beneath. Ryder almost felt sympathy for the man, until he remembered the pack's intention to kill him in the den, and the werewolf guardians' attempt to kill Vassi in the forest. The emotions he felt then were most definitely not sympathetic.

"Yes, yes, damn it." The man glared up at them, sweat running down the side of his face and neck.

"Were you working on your own, or under instruction?" Dave asked.

The lycan glared at the witch, his eyes glowing briefly. "Screw you."

Vassi sighed, and Ryder glanced over at her. Her expression was impassive, yet he could see the tight lines around her mouth, the shadows in her eyes. No matter how badass she presented herself, she didn't like this any more than he did. Dave, on the other hand, seemed to enjoy his work. They'd been at this for hours. The first time the lycan had lapsed into unconsciousness, Dave had given him some respite, going up to work on his client. There hadn't been much progress since Dave's return and, quite frankly, Ryder wasn't sure how much more Vassi could handle, let alone the lycan.

"May I?" he enquired, stepping further into the cell.

Dave gazed at him for a moment, before shrugging. "Sure. The more, the merrier." He rose from the wooden stool he'd been sitting on and handed the dagger and chalice over to Ryder.

Vassi frowned, but Ryder ignored her. So far he'd been quite restrained and on the defensive. He'd tried to run, hide and talk his way out of most situations with the werewolves, not wanting any more blood on his hands. Since the Woodland den, though, he'd realised that there was more going on than just a simple murder. Vassi just wanted to present benefit of the doubt, but he wanted more. For him to clear his name and stand any chance of surviving this ordeal, he had to find who was truly behind Jared Gray's murder.

Starting with this damn stubborn lycan.

"I'm going to assume that you weren't working on your own," Ryder began in a conversational tone. He set the chalice aside on the stone floor and leaned forward, the dagger dangling in a relaxed grip. The lycan glared at him, a wariness creeping into his gaze that wasn't there before. Good. So far everyone had underestimated him, but this lycan had seen what he'd done back at the Woodland den. He knew what he was capable of, and feared it. Ryder wasn't averse to using a little fear to his advantage.

"Wolfsbane is so dangerous, it's hard to come by, and most wolves won't go anywhere near it, let alone carry it in a box and deliver it." Ryder lifted up the blade and stared at it. "So someone told you to do it, and I have my suspicions, but I need you to confirm it. Who gave you the wolfsbane?"

The lycan bared his teeth. "I'm not telling you dick."

Ryder concentrated on the blade, calling forth a little lightforce, just enough to make the blade glow with heat. He ignored Vassi's gasp and thrust the dagger into the lycan's other thigh, and listened to the high-pitched wail as the lycan thrashed in pain. The smell of scorched skin wafted through the air. Ryder arched an eyebrow. Kind of like bacon.

"Feel that, lycan? That's your skin burning from the inside," he said, leaning forward until his eyes were on level with the pain-filled prisoner, letting the lycan see his determination, his ruthlessness. "I can make it stop," he murmured softly. "Hell, I can make it feel so good, you'll want to bottle it up and crack it open for Christmas, but you're going to have to tell me what I want to know. Otherwise I'll keep using you as a pin cushion."

He removed the dagger, then stabbed the lycan in the right shoulder. The lycan rocked back on the chair, screaming as the blade burned through tendon and muscle.

"Oh, God, okay," the lycan groaned. "I got it from Rafe."

Ryder nodded. He'd guessed as much, just needed to hear the lycan say it. "Why did Rafe want Jared dead?"

The man lowered his head. "This is pack business. I can't tell you."

Ryder twisted the dagger. "You made it my business when you brought your pack business into my clinic. Why did Rafe want Jared dead?"

The lycan gritted his teeth, the growl in his throat low and animalistic. "He didn't," he gasped. "We just wanted more land. We would have fought for it, but someone came up with this idea. We could either ask for a boon, or else take advantage while Alpine Pack sorted out who their new alpha prime would be. Either way, we could win."

Obviously they hadn't met Matthias, Ryder thought. From what he'd witnessed, the white wolf would ferociously defend the Alpine Pack. He frowned. There was something else, though, something possibly more disturbing. "Someone? Who?"

The lycan shook his head. "I don't know," he panted, sweat dripping off the end of his nose. "Neither does Rafe."

Ryder arched an eyebrow. "You don't know where the idea came from? Come on, you were ready to start tribal warfare and you don't know why?"

The lycan shook his head. "I swear, we just received encrypted emails from someone, we don't know who."

Ryder glanced over his shoulder at Vassi. The man's story was ludicrous, so ludicrous he had to wonder why he'd come up with such an outrageous lie and expect to be believed ... unless it wasn't a lie.

And his sexy little vamp seemed to have her own inbuilt lie-detector. Her eyebrows rose as she met his gaze.

"What?" she asked, her tone innocent.

"Is he lying?"

"How would I know?"

"Well, you seemed to have a pretty good idea back at the den."

She shrugged. "Hugo gave me a creepy feeling, that's all."

He rolled his eyes. "Rafe."

"Whatever."

"How is it that you get Dave's name right, but nobody else's?"

She looked at him as though the answer was obvious. "Because he's a Dave." She folded her arms, trying to avoid his gaze. "For what it's worth, this guy doesn't feel so creepy."

He stared at her for a moment, waiting for her to meet his gaze, which she did, reluctantly and ever so briefly. She was— scared. He blinked. She was scared, damn it. Of him? She'd already shown him her little skill, did she think he didn't know? Or maybe she didn't want him to know. He sighed. He didn't know why. Surely, after everything they'd been through, she knew he wasn't a threat to her. He'd just have to convince her that her secret was safe with him—later.

His gaze shifted to the witch leaning nonchalantly against the rock wall, who shrugged as well, only his attempt at looking innocent was almost laughable.

Ryder turned back to the lycan, frowning. So Woodland was behind the wolfsbane in his clinic. He could see what their gain would be, but who had put them up to it?

He leaned forward. "Where did you get the wolfsbane from? Or should I say, from whom?" Wolfsbane and verbena were hard to come by, the werewolves and vampires had tried to destroy all stock in an effort to eradicate the weapons that could kill them, but there were still places that some people knew of but most didn't openly talk about, where the poisons could still be purchased. His gaze slid back to Dave. Like witches.

The lycan shook his head. "I don't know." He cried out when Ryder twisted the blade again. "I swear, I don't know. My job was to deliver it to you. Rafe gave it to me. I think it was just delivered to us, we have no idea who sent it. It was better for everyone, that way."

"Better?" Dave asked, and Ryder sensed the witch's interest.

The lycan nodded. "Yeah. Better we don't know."

Ryder glanced at Vassi, who gave him that ridiculous wide-eyed stare, before she lifted one shoulder. "Again, not so creepy."

He finally nodded, satisfied he'd gotten as much information as he could out of the lycan. He called forth a flare of lightforce, sending it down the blade as he slowly withdrew it. The lycan screamed, then bellowed when Ryder pressed the scalding blade against the skin, sealing and cauterising the wound. He then pulled the power back within, and handed the cooled dagger back to Dave.

Dave arched an eyebrow. "You know werewolves self-heal, right?"

Ryder smiled. "Yes. But that will still leave a scar."

Dave nodded in approval, then strode over to the nearly unconscious lycan. He pulled a drawstring bag out of his back pocket and opened it, pulling out a pinch of herbs and waving it under the lycan's nose. The lycan startled awake at the scent, his pupils dilating until his iris was completely black.

"Do your thing, Vassi."

Vassi frowned, her hands going to her hips. "You had a compulsion concoction this whole time, and you're only now bringing it out? We could have used it hours ago and avoided all this," she said, waving a hand at the bloodied lycan.

Dave tsked. "Where's the fun in that?"

* * *

Vassi looked up as Dave entered the cavern again, dusting off his hands.

"Right. I dumped him a couple of blocks from here. When he wakes up he'll have no memory of what happened—or how he got his new scar. Oh, and here." The muscular witch tossed her a little pouch, and she glanced inside. A compulsion concoction, one to replace the lipstick Max had taken from her.

"Thanks, Dave," she said quietly.

"That should tide you over until you visit your mother. Best you do it before you get more lycans a-courting. Just remember, no compulsion spell can permanently wipe memory—a scent, a familiar sight—can always drag those hidden memories back."

She nodded. Perhaps that explained why Max remembered their kiss. She'd never kissed a liar more than once. Not until her client. "I still think we should have kept him."

"He's not a pet, Vass. He'd probably just pee all over the place and chew on anything he could get his teeth on."

She hadn't agreed with letting the lycan go, had wanted to keep him until they could get him to testify in court, but Max had insisted. He'd served his purpose, they had other avenues to pursue. She glanced over at her client, sitting at the wooden table Dave used as a witchy-woo cook-up counter. He'd surprised her—on so many levels.

When she'd first met him, he'd been in a vulnerable position. Handcuffed, wounded, yet he'd still had a mild strength about him. He'd allowed her to take charge of their situation, she recognised that now. She'd called the shots, but only because he let her. She'd seen that knife glow and didn't know what the hell to think. There was something hidden, something mystical about her 'mostly human' companion that both intrigued and frightened her. What she had considered a mild strength was more like an unbreakable wall of ruthlessness.

He'd been quiet since Dave had left with the lycan. She grimaced. She wasn't sure where they went from here. Someone had used Woodland Pack, just as they'd used him— but who?

"I'm not sure what the next step should be," she admitted into the cavern. Her client finally looked up at her, his blue eyes almost silver in the candlelight.

"The communication Woodland received was encrypted. Someone went to great lengths to coordinate this from a distance, and they would have taken every precaution. I don't think we'll be able to track them, they've been so sophisticated, they would have made those emails untraceable." He rose from the table. "We follow the wolfsbane."

Vassi frowned. "How? It's not like you can pick it up from the health food aisle at your local supermarket. I wouldn't know where to begin to look for something the werewolves have tried very hard to eradicate."

Max nodded. "True. We don't know. But you do," he said, shifting his gaze to Dave.

Dave stood with his feet apart and folded his arms, looking a little like a fallen angel with a bad attitude—and sunglasses. He smiled. "What's in it for me?"

Vassi rolled her eyes. She'd thought vampires were good at striking bargains to get what they want, but Dave put every vampire she knew to shame. Except for maybe Vivianne Marchetta, but she was in a league all on her own.

"What do you want?" she sighed.

"Same as before," he said, lifting his chin to Max. "Anything, anytime."

Vassi bit her lip. Owing two favours to a witch could be hazardous to one's health, but she had no idea how to progress from here, and neither did Max.

Max inclined his head. "Fine."

"Okay, then. You know the rules—" Dave started.

"Yes, we know the rules," Vassi interrupted. "No innocents are harmed—"

"And we do everything your way," Max finished dryly.

Dave smiled. "That's the spirit." He jerked his head back, indicating they follow him. "It's still daylight. We'll head out in the evening."

Vassi shook her head. "I'm good, we can go out now, if you like."

Dave walked down a tunnel, the occasional flaming torch casting a golden glow over his skin as he passed. "It's not for you, Vassi. The person we need to speak to won't be available until later. You guys may as well crash here for a couple of hours, then we'll head out."

He stopped in front of a large wooden door, banded with iron for extra support. He flicked his hand and the door swung open. Vassi gasped at the slight rushing noise, then the candles within the room flickered to life, revealing the interior of the room in a warm, intimate glow. Inside was a massive bedroom, with thick brocade drapes falling from ceiling to floor, masking the rock walls, a wardrobe and chest of drawers taking up space on one side of the room, and a very large bed in the middle of the room that looked like it could hold at least two Daves and maybe a bear like Taylor Henley.

She halted just inside the doorway as Max wandered around the room.

"There's only one bed," she whispered out of the corner of her mouth to her friend.

Dave snorted. "We're all adults here, Vass. You guys are jonesing so hard for each other I can practically smell it—and I'm not a shifter." He backed away from the doorway. "I'm heading upstairs," he said to Max, then held his hand to his mouth. "That way you can make as much noise as you want," he said in a stage whisper she was sure her mother could hear across town.

She closed her eyes in mortification as the bedroom door slammed, and Dave's annoying whistling slowly died away as he left.

She heard a breathy chuckle behind her, and turned to look up at the man who stood in the middle of the bedroom built for sin. Right next to that bed.

Chapter Twelve

"He's quite a character," Max observed as he slid his jacket off his broad shoulders, his blue eyes watching her.

"That he is," she said in agreement as Max strode over to the wardrobe and hung up his jacket, the muscles of his back and shoulders moving under the smooth cotton of his long-sleeved t-shirt.

"And quite the matchmaker, from the looks of things."

She frowned. "Yeah, although he likes to keep that side well-hidden, apparently." He'd never shown any inclination to set her up before now. She eyed the man across the room from her, the one that was watching her as intently as she was trying not to watch him.

"Must be the witch in him. You know how they like to meddle."

Vassi smiled. "That they do."

He took a step toward her, then another, his long legs easily shrinking the distance between them until he was standing in front of her. He tucked a strand of hair behind her ear, his gaze never leaving hers.

"So, what do you want to do?" his voice was like a low, sensual invitation, curling inside her with a slow warmth that was tempting to embrace. "Do you want to … talk?"

She blinked. Talk. "Yes," she said, clutching onto the lifeline he offered her. "Let's talk." She stepped away, shrugging out of her jacket and laying it along the top of the dresser. "Why don't we start with exactly what you did back there?"

He'd used magic, but nothing like she'd ever seen. Knowing he held that much power within, yet had never used it against her, was reassuring, but she'd still like to know what she was up against.

She pursed her lips. That sounded adversarial. She couldn't help it, her instinct for self-preservation was strong.

He smiled at her, his expression a little knowing, a little wicked. "Only if you share, too." He sat down on the bed and wiggled up against the wooden headboard. He even scooted sexily. Her heart was hammering in her chest, and she was desperately trying to hold on to the thought that this was her client. Handsome, darkly sexy, but her *client*.

He hadn't specified exactly what he wanted to share. She could work with that.

"Fine. So, how did you do that?"

He stared at her, his look calculating, before finally relaxing his shoulders. "I'm a light warrior."

Her eyebrows rose. Okay, so that wasn't what she'd expected. "I thought they didn't exist anymore."

His smile broadened as he lifted his hands, palms up. "Well, just like Old Irondell, we endure."

She shook her head as she stepped closer. "I thought you all died out with The Troubles."

He shrugged. "We came close. Decided it was best if everyone thought that."

She wracked her brain, trying to remember all the history lessons she'd sat through. "If I remember correctly, light warriors were some secret society that could use light as a weapon? And that during The Troubles there was so much political in-fighting that they ended up destroying themselves ...?" she asked, frowning with uncertainty. They had become but a footnote in history texts since the time of the Reformation.

Max grimaced. "Not quite. Yes, things got very heated. We were mercenary clans, and were hired for our skills in both warfare and medicine, and sometimes that meant light warriors were pitted against each other by their allies ..."

"So, like some fairy ninja?"

His brow dipped. "Again—not quite. But we learned that those for whom we fought viewed us as expendable commodities, collateral damage, if you will. They were happy to pit us against each other, and didn't really care that we were wiping out a race." He shrugged. "So we stopped."

Vassi blinked. "You stopped? Just like that?"

He inclined his head. "Well, it's a little more complicated. When we refused to fight, those who thought they'd bought our loyalty along with our force weren't happy. Every colony, pack, pride, sleuth, gang, flock, pod, etc. we'd ever worked for made it their mission to hunt us down. We were too dangerous to be left to our own devices."

She gaped. "You were hunted?"

"Not me, personally. My ancestors. We were driven into hiding. Fortunately we're good at evading hunters."

"Ah, like those guardians in the forest."

He smiled. "Yes. So now we don't advertise that light warriors still walk amongst the living."

"How did you escape the Woodland den?" She'd been trying to figure out how he'd done it.

"I just sent out a little blast. The shock of it knocks them out."

"A little blast," she repeated weakly. She'd felt the effects of that so-called little blast. She'd hate to see him make an effort. She was just beginning to see how dangerous he could be.

His mouth tightened as he correctly read her wariness. "I'm not a monster, Vassiliki. I'm a dentist."

She bit her lip. "Some might argue they're one and the same." He'd mentioned something about medicine. "How does all the healing fit into everything?"

He shrugged. "Like everything, there is balance. We can use our light to heal—or destroy." His expression saddened.

"I prefer healing people with my lightforce instead of—the other."

The other meaning killing them. Wow.

"So what exactly can you do?" she asked.

He smiled and waggled his eyebrows. "Oh, I can show you many things," he said in a low voice. He lifted a hand and snapped his fingers, and the room was cast into darkness. She gasped, trying to adjust her night vision. They were underground, though, and no light whatsoever filtered down to their level.

She sensed his presence behind her, then felt the warm caress of his breath against her ear. "To control the light, you need to love the dark," he whispered, and she shivered at the warm thrill that went through her at the seductive sound of his voice. A tiny little flame appeared in front of her. She gasped. It danced upon his palm, swaying and flickering to its own rhythm. She stared at it, mesmerised. He turned his hand gracefully, and she watched as the flame licked at his skin, yet left no mark.

With a snap of his fingers, the flame leapt across the room to dance from one candle to the next, leaving a path of golden light in its wake.

"It's beautiful," she breathed, as the room slowly lit up, like a dragon awakening from its slumber.

"It can harm or heal," he said. He turned her in his arms, lowering his head until he met her gaze directly. "Now it's your turn."

"Uh …" Oh, dear. She hadn't planned on actually doing any soul-sharing, but he'd just told her he was part of a race everyone thought had died out. She couldn't very well leave him hanging.

"I've entrusted a pretty major secret with you," he told her. "One that puts not only me but my whole tribe at risk. Surely you can tell me about your truthseeking."

Her eyes rounded. "How did you—" she began, then snapped her mouth shut. She'd pretty much shown him in the den. She hadn't intended to reveal her gift, but she guessed she'd been pretty obvious—and Max was many things, but stupid wasn't one of them.

She sighed. "Fine. I'm a truthseeker."

He smiled. "See, that wasn't so bad."

She lifted her chin. "I don't like people knowing," she said, lacing her tone with warning. It was a vulnerability that could be fatal.

Max nodded. "I once saw a truthseeker ripped apart at a corporate takeover when he highlighted a fallacy told by one of the CEOs." He tilted his head. "Does your law firm know?"

She shook her head. "No. Apart from various members of my families, nobody else knows." She grimaced. "Well, apart from Dave, apparently."

"You could earn quite a living with your gift," he remarked.

She laughed. "I could also paint a target on my back and walk down Main Street. Truthseekers are valuable until they're not. Then they're a liability that has to be neutralised."

Max frowned. "Is that how you see yourself? A liability?"

"No, but I understand some would definitely see me as a threat." She knew that from experience, had the talons to prove it. "Nobody likes to be called a liar, especially in front of others."

His eyes narrowed. "Can you compel the truth?"

She sighed. "No. I can sense deceit, but I can't make you tell the truth." She patted her pocket, the little pouch of herbs Dave had mixed for her a little bump in the fabric. "At least, not without help."

Understanding lightened his eyes. "Ah. The lipstick."

Her cheeks warmed as memories of kissing him in the hotel room resurfaced. "Yes. The lipstick you stole from me." The lipstick that was now lost, damn it. "So that's it. I know your secret, and you know mine." And each could cause the other irreparable harm if it was used against them. She wasn't sure what to think—this conversation could either solidify a connection—or give them a weapon to use against each other. The last time she'd revealed her secret, it hadn't ended well.

She turned away from him.

"Don't," he said, stopping her with a hand on her arm.

"Don't what?" she said, looking at him over her shoulder.

"Don't turn away, as though you're trying to hide it." He pulled her back to him, his hand reaching up to cradle her face. "You don't need to hide anything from me." He smiled. "Because apparently I can't hide anything from you."

"Oh, you can still hide the truth," she told him. "I can only tell that you're lying, I can't actually see your truth."

He pulled her into his arms. "Ask me something."

She arched an eyebrow. "Ask you what?"

He shrugged, a lazy glint in his eye. "Anything. Ask me anything."

She was so tempted—but she was his lawyer, and he was her client. This kind of flirtation, this kind of conversation and where it could lead—it just wasn't ethical. No matter how much she wanted to indulge her fantasies about this man, she couldn't. Shouldn't.

"What did you think of me when we first met?" Screw ethics. She was a lawyer. She had none.

He trailed his finger over her shoulder and down her back, and she shivered as her nipples tightened inside the lacy cups of her camisole. "I thought you were the most repulsive woman I'd ever met."

She blinked at the cool wash, then tried not to smile. "Liar."

He rested his hand on her butt, his head so close to hers, she felt the warmth of his breath down her neck and across her chest. "I thought you must have been the dumbest chick, taking my case on."

Cold tendrils embraced her. She arched her eyebrow. "I know what you're doing."

His blue gaze skimmed over her features before focusing on her lips. He cupped her butt and pulled her up against him, and she could feel the hard ridge of his arousal pressing against her. "I can't stand being this close to you," he whispered, lowering his mouth to hers. The chill of his deception was quickly swept away by the heat of his kiss. There was no hesitation, no tentative persuasion. His tongue swept into her mouth to caress hers as he pulled her close against him.

She tore her lips from his, panting. "God, Max. We can't. You're my client," she whispered, her gaze dropping to his mouth. He leaned forward, his cheek brushing hers.

"Ryder," he whispered into her ear before nipping her lobe.

She shuddered, her eyes closing as desire surged inside her. "I can't get involved with my clients," she said in an attempt to be good, to be strong—to deny herself the one thing she wanted more than anything else in the world ... the embrace of this man.

"Fine, you're fired," he muttered against her neck, then bit her lightly, before lifting his head to kiss her again.

Ethics, schmethics. She'd tried to be good, but he was just too good at tempting her to be bad. She entwined her arms around his neck, kissing him back. Her breasts rubbed against his chest. She moaned. She could feel her nipples caressing his ridges and bumps through their clothes. He picked her up, and she wrapped her legs around his waist as he walked backwards to find the bed and sit on it.

She straddled his legs as he ran his hands through her hair, pulling her head back so he could nibble on her neck. She trembled, enjoying the sharp pricks of pain, like a tiny burn before he licked it better, replacing the burn with the cool draft of his breath on wet skin.

His hands dropped to her waist, sliding under the fabric of her shirt and camisole. She shuddered at the warm contact, gasping as his hands rose up her back, his nails scratching her gently. She clutched at the soft fabric stretched across his broad shoulders, then grew frustrated by the barrier. Her talons slid out, just a little, and her breath caught at the pain of the injured one that scratched the inside of her flesh, and refused to engage.

Max pulled back, a small frown on his face. "What's wrong?" He grabbed her hand, pulling it back to see the tips of her talons—and the finger that remained unchanged.

"It's nothing," she whispered. "Just a by-product of the car accident. Forget it."

He tsked, then drew the finger into his mouth. She shuddered. She wasn't sure if the gesture was meant to soothe her or drive her insensible with lust. Oddly, it did both, the wet warmth easing some of the pain, yet the heat in his gaze as he met her eyes, slowly withdrawing her finger from his mouth—it was carnal and suggestive, giving birth to a curiosity to see just how steamy things could get between them. Her panties grew damp with her desire, and she twisted her hand out of his grasp and used her talons to shred his shirt from his body.

Desire flared even hotter in his gaze at her urgency, and he lifted her shirt over her head in one smooth movement, then tugged her down to kiss her hotly. She writhed against him, her need heating that secret cleft between her thighs as he slid his hands beneath her camisole. She moaned against his lips as his palms finally covered her breasts, the warmth pebbling her nipples with her arousal.

She trailed her fingers down his chest, relishing his strength. She flicked his nipple, then gasped, her head lolling back as he did the same to her. She squealed when he rolled her onto the bed. He caressed her shoulder, a finger playing with the thin strap of her camisole. She met his gaze, panting, then shuddered as he ripped the silk and lace from her body. His eyes flared as he gazed upon her breasts, and they paused for a moment, each taking their fill of the other.

He frowned, reaching out to touch the silver scars across her midriff and side. She bit her lip, waiting for some sign of distaste, of pity. He surprised her, leaning down to kiss the scars tenderly, one by one, then lifted his gaze to hers. There was so much compassion in his eyes, it was humbling—and reassuring. His gaze drifted over her body, and the warmth of compassion was slowly replaced by the heat of desire.

He reached for her with both hands, gliding his touch down her sides. She arched into his caress, moaning, then helped him undo the button and fly of her jeans. She kicked off her boots and lifted her hips as he dragged the denim and lace panties down her body, pulling her socks off along with them.

He stood, unzipping his jeans and hurriedly shucking off the rest of his clothes before joining her back on the bed. His muscles rippled with his movement, the corded strength breathtaking as he came to her. She sighed as his bare skin came in contact with hers.

So much heat, so much strength. He was hard against her soft curves. He kissed her thoroughly, his tongue rubbing against hers as he palmed her breasts. She moaned, trailing her hands over his back and shoulders as he kissed his way down her body to pay homage to her breasts.

He sucked one nipple into his mouth while he played with the other. She arched into his touch, trembling with need as he seduced her with his tongue and fingers with a carnal skill that left her breathless.

He switched his mouth from one nipple to the other, and she gasped as he bit the rosy peak lightly, then licked. She writhed as he kissed his way down further, nipping and licking a path of molten desire until he spread her thighs with his hands, keeping them apart with his broad shoulders.

His glance met hers briefly, between the valley of her breasts, and she shuddered at the hot look in his eyes. Her jaw dropped as the pale blue shimmered into silver and all of the candles in the room flared to life.

He dipped his head between her thighs and sighed, bathing her in his warm breath. She threw her head back and closed her eyes, then jolted when his tongue licked at her need, a strange heat rolling over her. She could feel his tongue sliding along the opening of her body, and could feel, almost taste her body against his tongue.

Her eyes shot open as he kissed her nubbin, feeling his lips, his tongue, his heat on her body, yet feeling the warm slickness in his mouth, confused yet delirious with desire until realisation dawned. She could feel what he felt. She didn't understand it, but the sensations bombarding her were both hers—and his. The pleasure she felt was doubled with his feedback, and she writhed as he sucked on her clit, exquisite bliss exploding through her. She moaned as he licked her gently, bringing her down from her orgasm with tender care, before waging a campaign of pleasure again.

Her eyes widened as his tongue flicked against her, and a finger slid inside her. Her thighs trembled, as yet again she was bombarded with dual sensations as he explored that hot, secret spot of hers. Her body clenched, and she not only felt her internal muscles tighten, she experienced it from his mind, the warm embrace of her body as it craved whatever he could give her. He kissed her thoroughly, down there, his fingers tweaking her desire until she closed her eyes and screamed as another delicious orgasm broke over her.

He lifted his head from between her thighs, satisfaction and hunger warring within his eyes as he kissed his way up her body. She enveloped him in her arms, his lean, muscular body covering hers. She arched her back as he slid inside her, inch by slow, tantalising wicked inch.

Her body was already so sensitised from what he'd done to her, she quivered in ecstasy as she sensed not only his body entering hers, but her body welcoming him. His silver gaze held hers as he slid home, her hips cradling his, his hands braced either side of her as he withdrew, and she moaned at the slick feel of his withdrawal, his pause, then his smooth glide in to the hilt.

His hips undulating in a sexy, steamy dance, he repeated the process, and she shuddered at the intense pleasure building in her body, building in his. His pace increased, his mesmerising gaze on hers as he shared his experience with her. She didn't know how the connection worked, didn't care, she just opened herself up to it, revealing the sensations, the tight need spiralling inside her, the climb from pleasure to heaven that was painful in its exquisite beauty.

It was too much. The heat, the light, the deep, deep pleasure. Her breath hitched, held, then she screamed as a blinding orgasm wrenched her away from sanity, her neck arching as wave after blissful wave crashed over her, over him. He shouted as he thrust into her, his hips flexing as he let go of his control and found his release. Over and over, the thrilling peaks were climbed, crested and climbed again until a bone-numbing satisfaction swept over them both.

He slid to the side and gathered her close. It took several moments for her heart rate to slow, for the pounding in her ears to recede, and for her toes to uncurl. She laughed breathlessly.

"Oh, my God," she gasped, "That was—" She stopped. Words failed her, but a mental fog started to lift.

"Uh-huh," he panted, grinning.

She laughed again. "I was wrong. Ryder does suit you."

Chapter Thirteen

Ryder awoke, recharged and revived. Sex had a way of restoring energy in a light warrior, but what he and Vassi had done far surpassed sex. He pulled her body close, all warm and soft in sleep.

He'd bonded with her. He hadn't meant to, but he'd found himself opening up to her as he'd made love to her, wanting to get inside her head and let her inside his. His arm stole around her waist, and he felt the faint ridges across her side.

Scars.

Since when do vampires have scars? Or talons?

He'd seen the vulnerability in her eyes when he'd touched the marks on her body. He'd been touched by her trust. Someone had obviously caused her great pain, someone she'd allowed to get close to her. She'd been so distrustful with him at first, so hesitant to share her secret. He valued the trust she'd placed in him, would treasure it, would defend it—and her—with his last breath.

Her breathing changed, and she wriggled her hips back against his as she slowly woke up. Arousal throbbed through him. He didn't think he could ever get enough of his sexy little vamp. He'd made love to her and wanted to do so again. And again, until they fell asleep again from sexual exhaustion.

She turned in his arms to look up him, her expression open and warm. "Hey, you."

He leaned down to kiss her slowly, then pulled back to look down at her. "Hey, you." He trailed his hand down her body and again felt the upraised skin. He frowned. "What happened here?" It wasn't just werewolves that could self-heal. Vampires could too, even half-bloods, if her recovery from the car accident was anything to go by.

"Nothing," she said, a slight mark appearing on her forehead. She turned fully to face him, effectively removing his hand from her stomach. "We should probably get up before Dave comes looking for us."

He arched an eyebrow. "Dave can wait until hell freezes over as far as I'm concerned." He slid his arm around her and gathered her against him. He didn't want to let her go, to lose this moment. He'd never felt so close to anybody else in his life.

"What happened to you, Vassi? And why does a half-blood have talons?" They weren't natural, they were an enhancement, probably installed by a miscreant surgeon.

"It happened a long time ago, Ryder, so long I've forgotten most of it."

Warmth flared within him at her use of his name. If he'd known a bout of lovemaking would make that happen, he would have done it much, much sooner.

"I don't believe you," he whispered against the top of her head before kissing it.

She pulled back to meet his gaze squarely. "If I tell you, will you tell me why you left your family?"

He arched an eyebrow. "You're beginning to sound like Dave, wanting something for something."

She smiled dryly. "That's the way of things in the miscreant world. There's always an agenda."

His eyebrows rose. "And what's your agenda?"

"Well, at the moment, it's trying to prove your innocence." She rolled away from him, dragging the sheet with her. The glide of cotton across his naked body was almost a caress, but he'd prefer the touch came from her hands, her body.

"Are you trying to avoid the question?"

She sighed, glancing back at him over her shoulder, her long dark hair cascading in waves down her back. "No, it's just difficult to talk about, sometimes."

His curiosity was mounting, but he wouldn't prod her. When she trusted him, she'd tell him. "That's fine." He leaned forward, sliding his arm about her waist and tugging her back into bed.

She nestled back against him. "When I was ten, I was visiting my father," she said quietly, and he stilled. "I got into a fight with one of my cousins, called him on a lie, told him I was a truthseeker, that I *knew* he was lying."

He hugged her closer, sensing her discomfort. He wasn't sure if it was from talking to him, or the topic of their conversation. Either way, he wanted her to feel reassured.

"He attacked me. He almost killed me. He was so much older than me, and stronger than me, and so angry and humiliated that I caught him in the lie. It took both my father and my uncle to pull him off of me."

"God, I'm so sorry, Vassi." It must have been incredibly traumatic for a child to be attacked by a vampire. At that age, a half-blood stood no chance against a miscreant.

"My mother was livid, and was so angry with my father. Once I'd healed from my injuries, she took me to a miscreant surgeon." She held up one hand, and gently extended her talons. "She never wanted me to be unarmed again."

Hell, no wonder she didn't trust anyone with her secret. Her own family had tried to kill her because of it. He kissed her shoulder.

She sighed. "Your turn."

He grimaced. Just talking about it dredged up bad memories, images that haunted him in his sleep, that attacked his conscience.

"My father has a gift for convincing people to do what he wants," he said quietly. He was glad she wasn't facing him. He was being honest, yet he still felt a compulsion, a misplaced loyalty to protect his family. "So does my brother, but he does things slightly differently. He can be … impulsive." God, that was a damn understatement. "He did something one day that I just couldn't forgive, and my father helped cover it up. I couldn't—I couldn't do it anymore, I couldn't live like that. Since then I haven't spoken to them and I don't want to. My brother hates me and I hate him. We can't be in the same room together. They can both rot, for all I care." Harsh words, and he meant every single one of them.

She rolled over to face him. "Well, aren't we an interesting pair. My family can't stand me because of how I am, and you can't stand your family because of how they are."

She'd said it so simply. He smiled. "Well, it's a good thing we can stand each other." He hadn't opened up to anyone like he had with Vassi. She did something to him, made him feel so weak, and yet so strong, at the same time. He didn't normally talk about his family, not to anyone, but with Vassi he felt like he could tell her everything. Almost. He leaned down and kissed her gently, feelings stirring within that were more than just physical passion.

She drew back, smiling at him. "We have to find out who gave Woodland the wolfsbane," she reminded him. "We're supposed to be in court tomorrow morning, and I'd like to have some information prepared for your defence."

For once, proving his innocence and clearing his name weren't consuming his thoughts and energy. "We have time," he whispered as he kissed her shoulder, smiling when he felt her shiver.

"No, we don't. You're on trial for murder, Ryder," Vassi said, cupping his face. Her brown eyes were solemn, carrying a dark weight that made him frown. "Do you know what a sentence would be like? You would be kept in a prison with other miscreants who have committed murder-across-kind. How long do you think you'd last once word got out that you were in for killing an alpha prime?"

"You sound like you care, Vassi," he said, gazing down at her. He could see her worry, her concern for him, and was touched.

Something flickered in her eyes, and she dropped her gaze. "I—I don't. I can't care about every case I catch, Ryder," she said. "I'd burn out. I just want you to realise how serious this is."

"Trust me, I know the severity of my predicament. I also know that you make a lousy liar," he breathed the words against her mouth, then took her lips in a kiss intended to distract her and himself.

His tongue tangled with hers as he pulled the sheet away from her body. Scooping her into his arms, he rolled onto his back until she straddled his hips, then rose up to a sitting position. He burrowed his hands into her silken hair, relishing the caress of her locks against the back of his arms as he cradled her head and kissed her. She tasted so darkly sweet. He ran his tongue over her teeth, enjoying the scrape of those cute fangs as her breasts rubbed against his chest. He moaned as her back arched, her hips undulating against his.

He lifted his head to catch a breath, and she smiled at him, a wicked lift of the lips that had his cock hardening in an instant.

She pushed him back down on the bed, kissing his neck and scraping the flesh there with her incisors before kissing a trail down one scar. He closed his eyes as those cute little fangs of hers nipped him gently on the nipple, before licking him better.

He was as hard as a rock, and rubbed himself against the damp core of her body.

"Uh-uh," she tutted, and he opened his eyes. "Now it's my turn," she whispered.

He grinned—then groaned as she nipped and licked her way down past his navel. She grasped him, and he hissed in pleasure as she stroked him from root to tip.

He could feel his power coiling inside him, woken to a lazy alertness. His lightforce surged through him, and he knew his eyes were changing by Vassi's gasp. He opened the bond, feeling it extend toward the woman who was now taking him in her mouth. He groaned, loving the wet warmth that enveloped him, sucking him, the sensations compounded by her experience, his hard strength throbbing in her mouth. She released him, stroking her hand up and down his length as she rose above him.

"How do you do that?" she whispered incredulously. "I can feel you feeling me."

"A benefit of being a light warrior," he murmured. He sighed as she lowered herself onto him. She gasped, her eyes widening as he slid inside her body. He gritted his teeth against the delicious sensation, her liquid heat surrounding him, her body clutching at him. He could feel with her the smooth glide of his body inside hers, how thick and hard he felt inside, throbbing against her internal walls.

He grasped her hands, entwining their fingers as he lifted his hips. She moaned, undulating her hips in a slow erotic dance that had him clenching his jaw to stop from exploding. Her breasts trembled with their movements, and she started to increase the tempo, her gaze locked with his as they exchanged sensations, strengthening the bond growing between them.

Seductive heat inside and out, he could feel her pleasure building, heightening, felt the walls around him tighten, heard her breath hitch, then her cry as her orgasm washed over her, and she bucked a little, her head thrown back as pleasure swamped her, swamped him.

He pulled her down and rolled over, pinning her liquid heat beneath him, and thrust into her, over and over, as he rode her convulsions to his own fulfilment. She gasped, her flesh highly sensitised, as once again tension started to build to another release, a flashpoint of passion that exploded through her, through him.

He growled as pleasure burst upon him, long and low, his hips flexing in tiny thrusts as he found his release.

He collapsed beside her, panting, and she lay there, trembling as their bliss slowly receded.

"That—that's incredible," she gasped. "Is that what it's like all the time for you?"

He hesitated. He didn't know how she'd react if he told her he'd bonded with her. He didn't want to explain what that meant, wasn't quite ready to face what that meant. "Uh, only on rare occasions," he prevaricated. Like, with a bonded mate. Yeah, not ready to face that just yet, not when he could potentially be sent to prison in a couple of days.

"I feel fantastic," she said, amazement in her tone.

He arched an eyebrow. "Don't sound so surprised."

She shook her head as she rose from the bed. "No, you don't understand. It's the same kind of feeling I get from blood. Like a little rush." She started to drag on her clothes, and sighed as she lifted up the remains of her camisole. It was less than a day old. She tossed the torn garment aside and dragged on her shirt, and his cock stirred once more when he realised she wasn't going to wear anything else under that shirt.

He rolled out of bed, dropping his gaze. Sexual energy was the purest form of vitality for a light warrior. With a bond connection, the intensity travelled both ways, doubling on itself. She felt energetic. He felt like he could take on the world. Yet if he tried to explain why Vassi felt so damn glorious, he'd have to explain everything else.

Not yet.

He pulled on his jeans just as there was a knock on the door. After making sure they were both decent, he strode to answer.

Dave stood on the other side, still wearing sunglasses, his arms folded, but at least he'd donned a black t-shirt and a leather jacket. "If you two lovebirds are done waking the dead, it's time to go."

Ryder glanced over his shoulder in time to catch Vassi's mortified gaze. Even from this distance, he could see the colour creep up over her cheeks.

"I'm so sorry, Da—" she started, and Dave held up a hand, grimacing.

"Ew, Vassi. Don't care." Dave shuddered, making a face.

The tall man strode away, and Ryder couldn't help the chuckle at their discomfit as he quickly shoved his feet into his boots and followed Vassi into the stone corridor.

* * *

Vassi gazed up at the store's sign. "Um, isn't that—" she began.

"Yep," Dave said abruptly.

They stood in front of the Better Read Than Dead bookstore. Although it was evening, there were still a lot of customers browsing the shelves inside. Even from the street, Vassi could see a small gathering on the mezzanine level for what looked like an author event. Busy night.

"Isn't that what?" Ryder queried. He stood on her other side, and she was supremely conscious of him. It seemed like her body had gone into high Ryder-alert, sensing his presence, his warmth. He'd had to borrow a shirt from Dave—and hadn't that been a mortifying moment, making that request. She looked at Ryder, and caught him staring at her chest before he finally raised his eyes to meet hers, and he grinned. Her cheeks warmed. It wasn't one of those oops, busted smiles. No, it was more of a I-know-what-you-look-like-naked-and-I-can't-wait-to-get-you-naked-again smiles. He didn't bother to hide his attraction to her, which just made her think of all the things they'd done to each other in the bed just under an hour ago, and all the things she still wanted to do with him. His lips curved as though he could read her mind.

"Dave's sister," she finally answered. Ryder's eyebrows rose as he turned his attention to the store window.

"*That's* your sister?" he said in surprise. The stunning redhead behind the counter smiled at a customer as she passed a bag of books over to them.

Vassi could understand his shock. Dave was tall, muscular, and had the look of a mean biker looking for trouble. His sister, Melissa, on the other hand, was tall and willowy, her vibrant red hair pulled back in a braid, her skin flawless. She was beautiful, angelic.

And she was a class A bitch. The woman had a thing against all vampires. Werewolves too—pretty much any creature that wasn't human.

"Seriously? Isn't there somewhere else we can go?" she asked her friend. His sister made no effort to hide her contempt for Vassi.

Dave shook his head and walked toward the door. "No. Mel doesn't just sell books. She's your number one source for all defences against miscreants. If the wolfsbane didn't come from her, she'll know where it did." The bell above the door jingled as he swung it open and stepped inside, Ryder close on his heels.

Vassi went to follow, but ran into an invisible wall. She frowned. Damn it. She glanced over at Melissa, who now stood behind the counter with her arms folded, a smug little grin on her face. Ah, now Vassi could see the resemblance.

"Can I come in?" Vassi asked. The property was warded. She'd need to be invited in.

Melissa smiled sweetly, then pointed to the sign behind her. The dark silhouette of fangs in a red circle with a line through it mocked her. "No, sorry," the redhead said, not sounding sorry in the slightest. "No vamps."

"Mel," Dave muttered, and Melissa shook her head.

"No, I reserve the right to refuse service. This is a miscreant-free zone." The woman leaned an elbow on the counter and cupped her chin in her palm as she smiled flirtatiously at Ryder. "Handsome, here, on the other hand, is more than welcome."

Vassi sighed as Ryder glanced at her in surprise. She waved a hand. "Oh, go ahead. I'll wait out here. She probably won't be of any help, anyway," she muttered.

Melissa made a face. "Bite me." She held up a hand. "Oh, wait. You can't—because you're not welcome."

"Mel," Dave said, resignation in his voice.

"Dave," she mimicked his tone. "I can't believe you still hang out with that trash."

"I can hear you, you know," Vassi called out.

Melissa smiled. "I know."

Ryder held up a hand, his gaze darting warily between the two women before turning back to Melissa. "I need to talk to you about wolfsbane orders."

Melissa's smile faltered for a moment, and her eyes hardened. She glanced around until she spotted a member of staff and beckoned them over to mind the till. She stepped out from behind the counter. "What do I get in return?"

Vassi rolled her eyes. Damn witchy demands. "What do you want?"

Melissa arched an eyebrow as she looked Vassi up and down. "I don't want anything from you." She turned to smile at Ryder. "But you, Handsome ..."

Ryder sighed. "What do you want?"

The redhead's eyes narrowed as she tapped her chin. "Hmm, what should it be? A lock of hair? A date?"

Vassi's eyes flared at the suggestion and Melissa laughed. "Well, isn't that interesting?" She tilted her head to the side. "Let's just leave it as an I.O.U.?"

Ryder rolled his eyes. "You are definitely Dave's sister."

She shrugged innocently. "Well, if you don't want my help ...?"

"I want it."

"Good. We should go downstairs," she said quietly, then smiled at Ryder and placed her hand on his arm as they walked between the stacks toward the back of the shop.

Vassi watched with narrowed eyes as the redhead glanced over her shoulder and shot her a smug smile before disappearing behind a door.

Bitch.

Chapter Fourteen

Ryder peered into the depths of the staircase. The place smelled like smoke—and brimstone. Melissa paused at the bottom of the stairs to pull out her keys.

"What's happened?"

Dave halted on the tread behind him, a slight frown behind the sunglasses he seemed to wear everywhere.

"Oh, just a little accident with a fire spell," she muttered. She tugged a torch out of her back jeans pocket and opened the door, gesturing for them to precede her.

The large room they entered was dark, with only light from the stairwell cutting a swathe into the darkness—and then she stepped into the room, switching on the torch and slamming the door shut behind her.

Ryder turned to her, seeing just enough of her beyond the torchlight to see the smile she'd been wearing was now gone. She raised a hand toward Ryder as a warm breeze lifted loose tendrils of her hair. She glared at him, her eyes narrowed as she started to mutter something incomprehensible, and then he felt it.

Invisible bonds sliding around his torso, trapping his arms against his sides. He hissed at the slow-building burn that roped his body, before glaring at the pretty witch who had seemed all flirty and light, but who now stared at him with a murderous glint in her eye.

"Who are you? What are you?" She bit the words out in a snarl.

"Let me go," Ryder said, calmly and succinctly.

"Uh, Mel …?" Dave asked. "What are you doing?"

"Who are you?" she repeated, and Ryder grimaced as the invisible bonds tightened, and the heat increased.

"I'm Ryder Galen, miscreant dentist."

"And?"

"And what?" he bit out. What the hell was wrong with Dave's sister?

"You come to my shop and ask about wolfsbane. I want to know who the hell I'm talking to."

"And I told you. My name is Ryder Galen and I'm a miscreant dentist." He tightened the muscles in his arms to get some room to move—to breathe.

"What the hell happened here?" Dave growled. Ryder looked over his shoulder, then gaped.

Light from the torch revealed a blackened room, the walls and floor scorched and scarred. The damage done was extensive.

Dave picked his way through the ashes and soot, kicking what looked like the leg of a table out of his way.

Melissa stepped away from Ryder, her eyes narrowed. "This is what happened the last time someone wanted to talk about my stock of wolfsbane." She folded her arms and glared at Ryder, then turned to her brother. "So why don't you tell me what the hell is going on?" The moment she turned away, Ryder summoned his lightforce, using it like a hot blade against the witch's magic. She cried out, stumbling, her hand to her head as he cut through her spell.

She turned to him, arm raised, her face pale, but he held up his hands in a defensive manner. "No, don't. I'm not going to hurt you, but I'm not going to let you bind me again."

"How did you do that?" she uttered the words breathlessly, rubbing at her temple, one hand still poised, ready for powerful combat.

"Let's just say you have your way of doing things, I have mine."

They stood there for a moment, each threatening to use power against the other, until Dave sighed.

"If only I had a camera to snap this moment and show you both how ridiculous you look." He brushed past Ryder. "Don't even think about hurting my sister." He held up a finger to his sister in warning. "Play nice, Mel."

Ryder slowly lowered his hands and the witch did the same, although her expression still showed her wariness. He turned about to properly look at the room, hoping she'd see that he was no threat to her.

Melted glass dotted the floor, and what had once been metal shelving now hung in a mangled mess from the walls. Debris littered the room.

"How long ago?" he asked quietly, walking further into the scene of destruction. The sulphuric stink was almost overwhelming.

"This morning," the redhead muttered.

"Doesn't look like the sprinkler system turned on," Dave commented, dragging a toe through the black ash on the floor. "Either a fault—or someone prevented it."

Melissa nodded. "The system was disabled. I had to use a dampening spell. I'm lucky the fire was only contained to this room."

Ryder's eyes narrowed. "Tell me exactly what happened."

Melissa put her hands on her hips. "Some guy turned up asking about wolfsbane, wanted to check out my stock, maybe order some. So I brought him down here," she said, gesturing to the room. "This is where I keep my store." She eyed Ryder. "I sell ingredients for potions, some tools for spells, that sort of thing. At least, I did."

"Like an apothecary?"

"Precisely. It's going to take me some time to clean up and build up my stock again." She pursed her lips.

"What about my black thorn, rue and willow order? And my ink?" Dave asked, frowning harshly.

She made a face. "It arrived this morning, up in smoke a few minutes later."

Dave swore and kicked something that clattered against the wall.

"He wasn't a miscreant, they're not welcome, so I thought he was safe." Melissa sighed as she stared at the destruction in the room. "If I ever see that bastard again, I'm going to set *him* on fire."

Dave nodded. "I'll bring the beer."

She high-fived him, then put her hands on her hips, her green eyes curious. "So why all the interest in wolfsbane?"

"Did you hear about Jared Gray's death?" Ryder asked, his attention again on the burn patterns along the wall.

Melissa snapped her fingers. "The Alpha Killer. I was trying to figure out why you looked so familiar. Personally, I think they should give you a medal for what you did, not a prison term."

He grimaced. "One, *I* didn't kill him, at least, not intentionally, and two—he was still a person."

She snorted. "You keep telling yourself that. The only good werewolf is a dead one."

He raised an eyebrow and glanced over at Dave. The big man shrugged. "She doesn't like miscreants."

He'd figured. Vassi was still standing outside the bookstore. He really wanted to get back to her. Thoughts of her, waiting for him—braless—were completely distracting. He turned back to the redhead. "Jared was poisoned in my clinic with wolfsbane. Personally, I don't touch the stuff, so I'm trying to figure out who is behind this whole mess."

She shook her head. "I don't take down every customer's name. I don't know who this guy was."

"What did he do, exactly?" Dave asked, leaning his hand against a wall.

"I showed him my stock, he made a selection, then I opened my ledger to record it," she said. "I'd turned my back for just a second, and then there was an explosion."

"An explosion?" Ryder stared around the room, then at the woman in front of him. "How the hell did you survive?"

"I'm a witch," she said simply. "It takes more than fire and brimstone to kill me."

Dave cleared his throat, and she rolled her eyes. "Fine, if you need to hear it. It worked"

"You're welcome," Dave said meaningfully.

"What worked?" Ryder asked.

Melissa wagged her finger. "Uh-uh. You don't need to know. I've learned my lesson. I'm not about to divulge my secrets to any more strangers."

"Yeah, because you were such a trusting soul before all this happened," Dave remarked dryly.

Ryder leaned over to look at the scorch marks that scrolled up the wall. There was a flourish to it, a weaving of marks that looked familiar. Suspicion, ugly and toxic, curled inside him. "Can you remember any orders for wolfsbane before the guy this morning?"

Melissa snorted. "I deal in herbs. There are a lot of folks out there who would like a little protection against the wolves. I sell plenty of wolfsbane—and verbena, along with lilies, oleander, nightshade, foxglove, hemlock, and all the silver and iron mineral compounds you could poke a stick at, just to name a few. There have been a lot of wolfsbane orders over the last few weeks. That Woodland Pack is determined to start a tribal war, and my human customers are stocking up for insurance."

"The guy who—" Ryder winced, "—firebombed your store. What did he look like?"

"Dark hair, brown eyes, tall—about your height," she said, eyeing Ryder. Her hand rose to toy with her braid. "Strong cheekbones, and the tiniest of little grooves in the corners of his mouth ..." she stopped, then frowned. "Er, or so I think. I didn't really pay that much attention to him."

"Liar." Dave looked at his hand, then grimaced, wiping the blackened soot onto his jeans.

Ryder's eyebrows rose. "That's actually quite ... detailed."

She shrugged. "If you think so. Does he sound like someone you know? I'd really like to get my hands on him," she muttered.

Dave made a choking sound and held up his filthy hand. "Please don't say anything more."

Melissa frowned. "I want to hurt the bastard. Look what he did to my store, damn it!" she turned to Ryder. "Do you know who he is?"

Ryder shook his head. "No," he lied. He looked over at her brother. "I guess this was a bust. Any evidence I had of clearing my name went up in smoke in the fire."

Dave sighed. "Sorry, mate. Wish it could have been otherwise."

Ryder gave them a half-hearted smile. "Thanks. Well, let's get back to Vassi."

Melissa made a face, but Ryder turned away before she could make another snide remark about his mate. He smiled briefly. Just the mention of her name had his body tightening in anticipation, his power rising like a lazy tide.

Then his smile died. But he had some business to attend to first. He started to climb the stairs.

* * *

Dave gestured to the stairs. "Perhaps Little Miss Horny Pants would like to go first?"

"I'm not horny," Melissa stated primly as she walked past him.

"Please, you're practically drooling over your flamethrower friend," he muttered. "You really need to start dating again."

She whirled on him, her green eyes flashing, and he knew he'd struck a nerve. "Look around you, Dave. Look what he did to my store. It took me years to build this. I can't find some of those herbs, anymore. This arsehole might just ruin me. I swear, if I get my hands on him …"

Dave grasped her wrist, raising it and sliding back the sleeve. "Then I'll have to add to this," he said, pointing to the intricate tattoo on the inside of her wrist. It was delicate, the dark flourish so visible against his sister's pale skin. He covered the mark and closed his eyes, sighing. "Thank God it worked."

"Uh, the fact that you're so relieved doesn't boost my confidence in your work, brother dear," Melissa said.

He laughed, opening his eyes to look into her clear green gaze. "Bitch." He let go of her.

"Prick." She turned back to the stairs, and hesitated. She glanced quickly over her shoulder. "Thank you."

He nodded, and they trotted up the stairs.

* * *

Vassi straightened from her position by the door as Ryder strode out of the bookstore. He grimaced and shook his head. "She couldn't help," he told her. "She's got no records, no information that might lead to an arrest."

Her shoulders sagged. "Damn. I'm so sorry. I actually thought for a moment that she might be of some help." She gave a half-hearted shrug. "Should have known better. We are talking about Melissa."

He looked up and down the street. "I think you should go stay with Dave for a couple of days," he told her. She frowned.

"Why?"

"I think he's more than capable of keeping you safe from any lycans."

"I see." She focused on her gift, letting it drift out and over the man in front of her.

"We have no other clues, nothing else to go on," he told her. The coolness of his prevarication snaked around her.

"I'm sure if we sit down and put our heads together, we'll be able to figure something out," she told him quietly.

He shook his head. "No, I don't want you involved in this, not anymore."

Her eyelids fluttered. There was no coolness there, just an honest warmth that chilled her heart. He didn't want her to help him.

"I'm your lawyer, Ryder. I'm here to help, that's my job." She glanced up as Dave and Melissa stepped out of the store. Ryder shifted to block her view, to return her focus to him.

Those dark brows were pulled together in a frown, his blue eyes sombre. "Not anymore. You're fired, Vassi." Implacable, resolute, encompassing, his brutal honesty surrounded her.

"Don't do this, Ryder. Not again." He was pushing her away. Again.

He touched her cheek, regret in his gaze. "I'm sorry."

He turned and strode away, quickly disappearing into the night.

Chapter Fifteen

"Whoa. Burned," Melissa commented with a mock grimace.

Dave arched an eyebrow at his sister. "Really? After what happened downstairs?" He shook his head, then turned back to Vassi, his sunglasses catching and reflecting the street lights. "Again? He's fired you before?"

Vassi's nodded as she folded her arms, hugging herself in the cool evening air. "Yeah, I think that was the third time."

"Three times since—" Dave cocked his head to the side as he made a mental calculation, "Friday morning?" He nodded. "Impressive work, Vass."

She rounded on her friend. "What happened down there?" Before he'd gone down there, everything had been fine. Hell, they'd been better than fine, especially after their 'nap'. He'd looked at her as though—as though she was important, damn it. Now, after spending ten minutes with a green-eyed witch, he couldn't wait to get away from her. She glared at Melissa. "What did you say to him?"

"Who, me?" Melissa fluttered her eyelashes innocently. "Perhaps he's just not that in to you?"

Vassi reached out, her movements a blur as she caught the witch by the throat and had her backed up against the building before Dave could stop her. The woman was taller than her, but Vassi still held her high enough off the ground that the witch's feet kicked ineffectually at nothing. Vassi let her eyes glow, and lengthened her fangs intentionally. "You're outside, Melissa. You don't have the protection of your damn store anymore. Don't try to piss me off unless you want to pay the consequences." She dropped the woman to the ground, and Melissa coughed, clutching her throat as she tried to force air back into her lungs.

"And you wonder why she doesn't like you," Dave said to Vassi, shaking his head.

"What happened in there?" She kept her tone calm, but her anger still showed in her eyes. Dave held out his hands.

"Calm down, Vass." He leaned over and helped his sister to her feet, then tightened his grasp when his sister tried to launch herself at his friend.

"It appears we weren't the first party interested in Melissa's sales records," he told her, and Vassi frowned as he set Melissa behind him with a warning look.

"Who else?"

"That, we don't know. Some guy pretended to be a potential customer and set fire to Melissa's apothecary."

Vassi closed her eyes in frustration. "And destroyed any record of who may have bought the poison," she said. Damn.

She glanced back down the street in the direction Ryder had walked. He'd come out, but hadn't quite seemed as defeated or lost as she would have thought. He'd just told her to back off, effectively.

"Look, you tried to help your client, and now he's fired you. Let's go back to my place and crack some beers."

She chewed the inside of her lip. "He only fires me when he wants to protect me," she said, then remembered the second time he'd fired her was in the bedroom in Dave's cave. "Or when he—" she stopped when she realised what she was about to disclose.

Melissa's eyebrows rose in question, but Dave screwed his face up and clapped his hands over his ears. "Don't want to know, Vass. Don't care. La la la."

She blushed. "Well, you get my drift."

Dave dropped his hands. "I so wish I didn't."

Vassi put her hands on her hips and walked a few steps. "So someone definitely ordered the wolfsbane from Melissa, and burned her store so that nobody could trace who was responsible." She frowned again. "The werewolves, covering their tracks?"

Dave shook his head, and lifted his chin at the sign inside the store. "No miscreants allowed, remember? They can't enter without Melissa's permission."

She shot his sister a dark look. "How could I forget?" She turned and walked back toward him. "So, if it wasn't a lycan, who burned the store?"

"Woodland want to expand their territory. They could have any number of unknown allies," Dave suggested.

Vassi bit her lip. "Maybe we're looking at this from the wrong angle?" she lifted her gaze to meet Dave's. "We've looked at this as a murder, and focused on the victim—who had the most to gain, who had a grudge, etc."

Dave arched an eyebrow. "Isn't that how you normally look at a murder?"

She lifted a hand. "Well, there could be another victim, here." She stepped closer to her friend, her earnest reflection staring back at her from his sunglasses. "Who suffers if Ryder is convicted of murder?"

Dave frowned. "Well, Ryder, I guess."

"Exactly. We've been looking at this case from the perspective of Ryder being used to kill Jared. What if we looked at it from the perspective of Jared being killed to strike at Ryder?" Her eyes widened. "We're looking at this whole thing wrong. Jared was the weapon to get at Ryder."

Melissa pressed her palm to her forehead. "You're making my head ache."

Vassi pulled her phone out and noticed she only had one bar left on charge. She quickly dialled her assistant, putting the phone on speaker and holding it between her and Dave, her heart thumping.

"You called, oh sexually stunted one?" Seraphina answered, and Vassi closed her eyes as Melissa laughed.

"You're on speaker, Sera," Vassi informed her. "I need you to do me a favour. I need you to do a background check on Ryder."

"Uh, I already did. Sent it to you Friday, with all the case notes. How is our hunky client going? Let him into your volcanic snatch yet?"

Dave raised both eyebrows and looked at her, and she frowned. "Uh, not really the time, Sera. I mean a check on who benefits from Ryder going to prison."

"You know it's Sunday night, right? That some of us have a smoking hot social life and don't sit around waiting for your call?"

"Seraphina," Vassi growled.

"Fine, fine," her assistant muttered. "But I want you to know that you are interrupting something magical."

"Delayed gratification can be character building," Dave commented in a low drawl, and Vassi's eyes widened. Was he flirting with her assistant?

"Oh, baby, I'm great at building character," Seraphina cooed back, and Dave chuckled.

Vassi shuddered. "Uh, back to work," she said. "I need to find out what happens to Ryder's assets if he goes to jail." Another thought occurred to her. "Or if he's killed by the lycans in a tribal law act."

"Okay, give me a second," Seraphina said, then giggled and whispered something to someone in the background. In a moment Vassi could hear the tapping of fingers on a keyboard. "Okay, so I'm in the public trustee's database, just let me pass these security gateways ..."

Vassi grimaced. "You shouldn't tell me you're hacking into a government site," she told her assistant.

"Did I mention anything about hacking? Besides, that's a crude and violent term. I like to think my work is much more delicate and skilful."

"She's really hacking into a government database?" Dave enquired, and Vassi winced. "That's so sexy."

"Oh, honey, you ain't seen nothing yet," Seraphina purred. "Okay, so looking up—oh, wow."

"Wow? What's wow?"

"Did you know Ryder had a mother?"

Vassi arched an eyebrow. "I assumed he came into the world much like we did."

"No, I mean his mother was loaded. She left him and his brother a tidy little sum of money and some real estate. If Ryder was to die, it reverts back to his family. That is, to his father and brother."

The family he'd walked away from.

"Can you send me photos of them, and their addresses?"

"Sure. I can send you one of me, too, if you like."

"Yep," Dave responded instantly.

"Just the Armstrongs, please Sera. Thanks." Vassi disconnected the call and shot Dave an exasperated look.

He grinned. "She sounds cute. Fix me up with her."

"No."

"Come on, you owe me one."

She smiled sweetly. "Actually, Ryder owes you two. I don't owe you anything." Her phone beeped, and she quickly pulled up the messages from Seraphina. The images came through of Ryder's family. She easily recognised Arthur Armstrong. She flicked through until Ryder's brother's image popped up. Hunter Armstrong was a good-looking man. Dark hair, dark eyes, she could see the family resemblance. Though Hunter was handsome, he didn't arrest her attention like his brother did, with his stunning blue eyes and a protective streak a mile wide.

"Let me see that," Melissa breathed, grabbing Vassi's wrist. Her eyes narrowed. "That's him. That's the guy who blew up my store."

And now Vassi knew why Ryder had fired her—again. He was going up against another light warrior.

The next message from Seraphina showed an address. "I'm going," she told Dave.

He stared at her for a moment. "I'll help."

She tilted her head back. "I didn't ask for it."

"I'm offering," he told her. She looked at him, his features hidden by his sunglasses. Offers for help required no payment. He couldn't demand anything in return.

"Why?"

He leaned forward. "You're my friend, Vass. You don't know what you're up against. This guy obliterated my sister's store. You're going to need a witch on your side."

"Make that two," Melissa stated. Her expression was resolute.

"Oh, no," Vassi said, shaking her head. "Not you. You can stay here." She'd spend most of her time watching her back if the green-eyed witch joined them.

Melissa gave her a dangerous smile. "I'm coming with. I have a score to settle with this bastard. He tried to kill me." Her smile broadened. "If there's one thing we witches do well, it's revenge."

"You can't kill him," Vassi warned. "We need him to prove Ryder's innocence."

Melissa inclined her head. "Fine. I won't kill him—until after Ryder's free."

Vassi narrowed her eyes and looked at Dave, who grimaced. "I wouldn't try to stop her. She'll just do a locator spell." He turned to his sister and held up a finger in warning. "Play nice."

"Or what?" she challenged, folding her arms and lifting her lips in a smug smile.

Dave smiled right back, showing his teeth. "Or I'll tell Mother."

Melissa stopped smiling.

* * *

Ryder gripped the lock on the gate. He wanted to blast his way into his brother's compound, cause as much damage as possible, but he still had enough control to realise that subtlety had its good points—namely, not alerting his brother's guards. No, now was not the time to give into the rage coursing through his body. He banked the angry fires within, using a cool detachment his father had instilled in him to manage his emotions—something he'd hated at the time, but now acknowledged a use for.

He pressed the eight-digit code into the security keypad, surprised when it worked. He co-owned the mansion, had lived here with his brother up until six months ago. He'd thought Hunter would have changed the code by now. His mistake.

He pushed the gate open and glanced across the manicured garden. Guards patrolled the grounds, and he watched as two turned a corner, weapons held at the ready. Ryder veiled his body's outline, gathering and dispersing light particles around him, reflecting his surroundings until he became invisible, then strode up the garden path, around the tinkling fountain, its water sparkling in the moonlight, until he reached the door. The home was protected against intrusion from others—except light warriors. He tapped in his code, smiled with satisfaction when the light changed to green, then slid unobtrusively into the home he'd once shared with his brother.

Walking quietly down the wide hallway, Ryder held his breath, trying to gauge where his brother was inside the mansion. There was a clink of glass, the sound of liquid being poured. Ryder's lips twisted. Hunter was in the library.

Muscles in his jaw ticked. His brother was enjoying a drink in the library, while he ran for his life from a whole tribe of lycans.

He stalked down the entry hall on silent feet, down the three steps into the reception parlour, then across the room until he stood at the library door. He grasped the handle, then paused, taking a deep breath. Anger at what his brother had done swirled through him, almost blinding him. He'd killed

Jared Gray. He knew his brother's talents. He had the skills to manipulate an alpha prime and his pack, he knew the toxins, knew how to get hold of them—and would be prepared to take whatever action necessary to cover his tracks, including the attempted murder of the lawyer charged with defending Ryder's innocence, his bonded life mate.

Screw detachment.

He summoned a surge of lightforce, just a little, and the door burst inward, splinters flying like an upset case of toothpicks, the rest of the wooden shards bursting into flame, quick and intense, before turning to ash.

The man standing by the fireplace looked up from his drink and arched an eyebrow.

"Hello, brother."

Chapter Sixteen

Vassi peered between the wrought iron rails of the gate. The moonlit gardens were a contrast between silver and darkness, and it took her a moment to spot the two guards standing by a bush, each taking a drag of a cigarette.

She pulled back and turned to the two witches behind her. Dave was using a small bottle of henna ink to draw a design on the back of Melissa's neck, muttering something incomprehensible as he did so. The ink glowed, the design shimmering for a moment before lapsing into a dull brown. The intricate design was beautiful.

"Okay, there are two guards, I can't see any more. I'll go in over the wall and take them, you wait here until I give the all clear," Vassi whispered. She was faster than either of the witches.

Dave shook his head, then fanned the temporary tattoo he'd drawn on his sister. "No. You know my rules. No innocents are harmed, and we do this my way." His voice was low, his tone implacable.

"You think those guards are innocents?" she hissed at him.

"We can see they're not miscreants," he retorted. "They're armed. If you can drain someone's blood or attack them with your teeth, you don't need a gun. These guys are just doing their job, Vassi. Nobody should die for just doing their job."

"Well, how do you propose we get in there?"

"That's easy," he whispered. He reached beyond her and nudged the gate. It moved on well-oiled hinges, and she gaped.

"Oh. I hadn't noticed that." And here she'd been mentally planning her assault to the tune of Mission Impossible.

"Looks like lover boy is here already," Dave murmured.

She wanted in, desperately. Ever since they'd set out this evening, she'd been focused on Ryder. He consumed her thoughts. Her need to see him, to touch him, drove her to distraction. He'd pushed her away, yet again. She understood, but she damn well didn't agree with it. Sooner or later he was going to have to trust her to have his back, and to be able to protect her own. They'd faced everything together, devised their plan of action together. Being excluded from his thoughts, from his plans, stung. It triggered memories of the way her family treated her—cautiously, warily, waiting for her to fall below their low expectations, to cause them extra trouble, extra effort, perhaps even extra heartache.

She tightened her lips. She knew he wasn't doing it for those reasons, but the effect was the same. He didn't trust her. The problem was, he'd need her help, damn it. She wasn't just a court officer any longer. After the Woodland Pack attack, she was a witness. She could now offer some defence for him—as long as he didn't kill his brother.

If he did, then it didn't matter what trick she pulled out of her hat, he'd be going to prison.

She turned to Dave. "What if I just nipped them? Drain them until unconsciousness, then we can go on our merry way, no innocents harmed."

Dave frowned. "You're not going to bite anyone, Vass." He glanced at his sister. "Besides, we have a painless weapon."

Melissa nodded, then untied the band around her braid, fluffing her hair out until it fell below her shoulders in a soft cloud of red curls. "Watch and learn, vamp. This is how you get a guy into you."

She undid the top three buttons on her shirt, adjusted her breasts, then pushed the gate open and strode in.

"Hi boys, can you help me? I'm on my way to a party and I'm tragically lost."

Vassi blinked as Melissa strode down the path, her hips swaying in her tight jeans, shoulders back. Even her voice, low and sultry, was different to the shrew Vassi knew and loved to hate.

The guards hurried over. One bore an eager expression, the other looked vaguely suspicious. Melissa tripped, her hands flashing out to grab hold of each guard's arm to steady herself.

"Phew! These heels are a killer," she laughed, sounding relaxed and possibly just a little inebriated. She tilted her head back, a smile of pleasure on her face.

"She seems so nice," Vassi whispered in amazement.

Melissa started to chant, her eyes closing as she kept her grip on the guards, and suddenly both were writhing, clutching at their heads and trying to loosen Melissa's grip. One fell, and then the other, unconscious on the stone paving. She brushed her hands together as though dusting herself off.

"And then she's not," Dave said, breathing a chuckle as he entered the garden. Vassi followed him, eyeing the guards warily.

"What did you do to them?" she asked the redhead.

Melissa smiled. "They're just napping, having some pleasant dreams."

Dave arched an eyebrow, and his sister shot him an innocent look. "I promise, no nightmares, just some sweet dreams."

"How long will they be out for?" Vassi asked, prodding first one with her toe, then the other. They were definitely out cold.

"Long enough," Melissa responded tartly. "Their boss will be dead by the time they wake up."

"Why does she get to kill someone and I don't?" Vassi muttered as she followed Dave up to the front door.

"Because the guy she wants dead tried to kill her. That's fair. Everyone else just happens to be in the wrong place at the wrong time. Not so fair." He halted at the door, then frowned. "This is unlocked, too."

"This has got to be the easiest intrusion I've ever done," Vassi observed, then met Dave's curious gaze. "Not that I've tried this sort of thing before," she said hurriedly.

"Well, I have, and you're right. It is easy. Maybe too damn easy."

"I don't care," Melissa hissed behind them. "The night's a-wasting. Let's move."

She pushed the door open, then huffed when Dave dragged her back behind him and entered the hall.

Vassi tried to follow and met that immovable, unseen wall. She bit her teeth as Dave and Melissa entered the home.

"Wait, I haven't been invited in," she whispered.

Dave frowned. "You'll have to wait there, then. We'll take care of this."

Melissa gave her a cheery little wave and turned to follow her brother. Vassi eyed the entry for a way in, frustration biting at her, as the two witches strolled further into the house.

The large front door swung open into a brief hallway that led to a step-down lounge room of sorts, from what Vassi could see. She ran back down the front steps and scurried along the path to the next window to peer in. There was a fire going in the large, recessed hearth, and wall sconces and a chandelier cast a golden glow over the room. Wooden balustrading gleamed along the upstairs hallway that looked down on the room, and big stuffed settees sat opposite each other. Dark wood and exposed beams gave the cathedral ceilings a gothic vibe, and Persian carpets in red tones covered the dark timber floor with an opulent masculine air.

She watched as Dave and Melissa paused in the room and looked around. Where were Ryder and his brother, Hunter?

A flash of light, followed by a loud bang, came from a room off the parlour, splintered wood lying around the entry. Dave and Melissa ducked, then cautiously hurried over to the doorway. Vassi swore quietly. She couldn't see into the room. She stepped back and hurried along the path until it turned the corner of the house. Keeping an eye out for any more patrols, she ran hunched over alongside the house until she reached another window. The room inside was dark.

Damn. She bent low, using the box hedge as cover to get to the next window, then peered inside. She gasped. The window was open, and she could clearly see and hear the goings on.

Ryder was on his back on the floor, a dark-haired man wrestling on top of him. Vassi clenched her fists. She couldn't get inside, damn it. She pulled her mobile phone out of her pocket, then groaned. No charge. Damn it. She couldn't call for help, couldn't get inside. Not until the owner of the house invited her in. Ugh. It was so damn frustrating. She wanted to go in there and help her man—no, she *needed* to go in there and help her man. She'd never felt this strange compulsion to be so close to another, to put herself at risk for another, as she did for Ryder.

Ryder roared, and the man he was fighting flew across the room, hitting the bookcase with enough force to break two shelves, books cascading down like a waterfall. He fell to the floor, but quickly got to his feet, as did Ryder.

"You're trying to get me killed, Hunter," Ryder roared at his brother.

"I think you're accomplishing that on your own, brother dear," Hunter yelled back. Head down, he charged at Ryder, tackling him up and over the reading desk. One of them, Vassi wasn't sure which, kicked the desk lamp, and both Melissa and Dave ducked to avoid the missile. Dave met her gaze across the room, one hand facing out to her, the other pressing a finger to his lips.

Vassi's lips tightened. Hold and stay quiet. God, she didn't think she could just stand by and watch Ryder face his dangerous brother.

"You destroyed the apothecary," Ryder said in a harsh voice as his brother tried to strangle him. Vassi reluctantly nodded. Maybe Ryder could get a confession out of his brother. With Dave and Melissa as witnesses, letting these brothers have at it could clear Ryder's name. She didn't like it, though.

"I had to, to cover up your mistakes, you idiot," Hunter rasped, then howled when Ryder used both hands to punch him in the chest. Vassi's eyes widened as she saw the light flare, and then Hunter was tossed back against the shelves again. This time it took him a little longer to gain his feet, the front of his shirt smoking.

"You can't stand that I walked away," Ryder gasped as he sat up on the desk. "You couldn't just leave it alone."

"Oh, please," Hunter scoffed. "You shamed the family, Ryder. You broke Dad's heart. If I 'left it alone'," he said, using his fingers to parenthesise the air, "we'd probably all be in jail."

"Dad's heart was broken long before I left, Hunter."

Both brothers glared at each other for a moment, breathless, sweaty and bleeding from small cuts.

Ryder rose to his feet. "Is this about Debbie?"

Hunter halted, his features screwed up as he met his brother's glare with perplexity. "What? Debbie? No. This is all about you, you douche."

"You hate me so much?"

Hunter put his hands on his hips. "Actually, now that you mention it, hate doesn't quite cover it." He cupped his hands, and an orb appeared above it, which he promptly hurled across the room.

Vassi clapped her hand over her mouth as the power blast sent Ryder flying back over the desk and into the chair behind. The chair collapsed under the force of the hit, and Ryder groaned as he rolled off the debris. Hunter nodded. "That's for Debbie."

Ryder coughed as he staggered to his feet. "How many times do I have to apologise for that?"

"I loved her, damn it. You should have let her go."

Ryder swore. "I loved her, too," he yelled back.

Vassi gaped as the brothers glared at each other. Who the hell was Debbie?

* * *

Ryder closed his eyes. Damn it. It was one of those things that festered between him and his brother, like an infected blister ready to spew forth rancid emotion at the slightest pressure.

"We both loved her, but we both couldn't have her." There was so much pain, so much antagonism between the two of them now. All because they'd loved the same woman.

Hunter turned away from him. "Well, the favoured son strikes again. First Dad, then Debbie. You got everything, then you threw it away."

Ryder shook his head. "I didn't throw anything away."

Hunter whirled on him, his expression raw with pain. "You threw her away. You let her *die*." He flung another blast that caught Ryder and threw him against the side of the fireplace.

Ryder grunted, then pulled himself up by clutching the mantelpiece. Hunter stalked toward him, his hand in front of him.

"She had to decide, and she chose you. I get it." Hunter's shoulders sagged. "Damn it, you were supposed to take care of her." The words were softly spoken, but carried so much pain.

"I couldn't protect her from you."

Hunter's chin jerked back, as though struck. "What?" His voice had gone lethally quiet.

"I'm sorry," Ryder whispered. "You don't know the full story, Hunter."

Hunter held out his arms. "Well, by all means, brother, enlighten me."

"She was already chosen for me, Hunter. Dad saw to that."

Hunter's eyes narrowed. "What do you mean?"

"You know what he does, Hunter, don't tell me you don't." Their dearly beloved father enjoyed manipulating people, including his sons, pitting one against the other to see who was the stronger, over and over. He'd done it for as long as Ryder could remember. He had a special talent in that area.

"What does Debbie have to do with what Dad does?"

"Yes, Ryder, what does Debbie have to do with me?"

Ryder glanced over his brother's shoulder. His father stood in the ruined doorway, his eyebrows raised. He was dressed in a tux, a handsome, middle-aged man-about-town. He bent down and righted a chair, then draped his overcoat over the back of it. He turned to his sons with an expectant look on his face.

"Does somebody want to tell me what the hell is going on here?"

Chapter Seventeen

Vassi ducked below the windowsill, her eyes wide. Good grief. Arthur Armstrong, in the flesh. Was this a good or a bad thing? She remembered all the stories and rumours she'd heard about Arthur Armstrong, and his son Hunter. She shuddered. Okay, maybe not so good. Where were Dave and Melissa? Had they hidden, or had Arthur found them? She hadn't heard any scuffle from outside the room. Knowing Melissa, she wouldn't have gone quietly. Neither would Dave, not without a fight. So, maybe they hid? God, she hoped they hid. There were three light warriors in the room. The odds weren't good for any of them, and the two witches had no idea what they could be up against.

She clenched her fists. She was still reeling from discovering Ryder had been in love before. It shouldn't be such a surprise, really, but the raw pain in his voice when he spoke of this Debbie, the agony lining his face … it struck at her heart, and she didn't know if she felt anger, or jealousy … or envy. She just knew she wanted to clasp him to her and kiss him until he forgot about this woman, until he focused on her, focused on the present, and perhaps a future. She sighed. Perhaps she wasn't as evolved as she thought she was. Plain and simple, she wanted Ryder's devotion directed at her, not a ghost.

She peeked up over the windowsill again.

Ryder heaved away from the mantelpiece. He was frowning. She bet he hurt. They both should, after the punishment they'd been meting out. He lifted his chin and stared at his brother. "Didn't you ever wonder about Debbie coming to that Halloween ball? Neither of us knew her. Dad invited her."

"She was the daughter of Dad's business associate," Hunter shrugged. "So what?"

"We are so different, you and I. Didn't you ever wonder how we could fall in love with the same woman?"

"She was Debbie. She was ... amazing."

"I know, but she was amazing to you, and amazing to me." Ryder shook his head. "We couldn't even agree on the same radio station in the car, Hunter." He pressed his finger to his temple. "Think about it."

"You both fell in love with the same woman. It happens." Arthur Armstrong grimaced. "I wish it hadn't. She drove such a wedge between you both, and despite all my efforts, I still can't get you to forgive and move on."

Ryder didn't acknowledge his father's comment. "We fell in love with the same woman because Dad wanted us to." Ryder clenched his fists. From what Vassi could see, the tension in his arms, his shoulders, his lips, Ryder looked like he wanted to beat some sense into his brother.

Hunter shook his head. "Oh, Ryder. You really have lost the plot, haven't you?"

Arthur made a noise of disbelief.

"Stop it," Ryder snapped, his gaze darting between brother and father. "For once in your life, try to get an original thought in your head that hasn't been planted by Dad."

Hunter smiled nastily. "Fine then. Dad introduced both of us to the same woman, probably hoping one of us would at least get her." Hunter stopped smiling. "And then one of us did." He stepped closer. "Dad can't compel us, Ryder. He didn't make us both fall in love with her."

Ryder clasped his hands together and touched his nose. "No. No, he didn't compel us." He lowered his hands, meeting his brother's gaze. "He compelled Debbie."

Hunter froze, his eyes searching Ryder's face. "What?"

"Ryder, that's ridiculous," Arthur admonished as he stepped closer.

"When she was dying, Hunter, she said something to me ..." Ryder swallowed. "She told me it wasn't real. None of it was real."

Hunter ran his hand through his dark hair, his expression dark with pain, with confusion. "What the hell is that supposed to mean?"

"Perhaps she was talking about her love? I will admit, I didn't like the woman. I didn't like the way she manipulated you two." Arthur folded an arm across his chest and braced an elbow on it, then rubbed his chin. "I never understood how one woman could love two men at the same time."

Vassi grimaced. His father sounded caring and disappointed, yet still managed to turn the knife in both sons with his observation.

Ryder folded his arms. "She was my perfect woman, Hunter."

Hunter's jaw flexed. "She was mine, too."

God this was painful to hear. Vassi blinked and looked away. This undying love for another woman, this worship ... she hated listening to it, but couldn't drag herself away from the moment. She glanced back inside the room.

"Exactly," Ryder said, almost triumphant. Vassi's brow wrinkled in confusion as he cocked his head to the side, his blue eyes so pale in the muted light of the fireplace. "She was precisely what each of us wanted in a woman—but we don't want the same thing, do we Hunter? She was different with me than when she was with you."

"Of course she was," Arthur said with a sigh. "She was using you both."

"No." Hunter shook his head and backed away. "No. She came to see me that morning."

Ryder clasped the mantelpiece. "What? You never told me this."

Hunter smiled, but there was no humour, no softness in the movement. "She was dead, what was the point?"

"Why did she come see you?" Ryder asked. Vassi held her breath, as interested in Hunter's response as Ryder seemed.

"She came to tell me she'd made a mistake," Hunter said quietly. "She said she'd chosen the wrong brother."

Ryder frowned. "That's—it doesn't make sense."

Hunter scowled. "What? That perhaps someone would actually choose me over you?" Hunter's lips twisted. "Do you find it so difficult to believe someone actually loved me? You were Dad's favourite son. Mother's too. Debbie loved me. She was going to leave you, for me."

"Hunter, that's not true," Arthur said, frowning. "You know I have no favourites."

Hunter turned on his father. "Really, Dad? Still? Ryder can walk away from you, from the family, from everything we've worked so hard to build, while I stand by you, I work with you, I'm still here—and you don't have any favourites?" Hunter shook his head in disgust. "Your own son abuses his girlfriend, and yet, I'm still so much lower on the totem pole."

Ryder shook his head, his disbelief obvious, and Hunter struck out in anger, sending a vase flying across the room to smash against the wall. Vassi flinched at the violence. "She was afraid of you," Hunter bellowed.

Ryder's eyes widened. "No. I loved her. I would never do anything to hurt her. She knew that."

"It happened so long ago, we should move past this," Arthur said, extending his arms out in each direction to his sons. Neither paid him any attention.

"She was afraid of you, and she was leaving you. And then she wound up dead on the driveway," Hunter thundered, his arm gesturing toward the front of the house.

"Because you put her there," Ryder yelled, jabbing his brother in the chest with a finger.

Hunter stepped back, his expression an almost comical mixture of shock, disbelief, then rage. "You did, brother," he yelled back, and hurled a blast of power at his brother. Vassi cried out as Ryder was flung into the fireplace. She moved toward the window, but still met the invisible force that prevented her from running to her lover's side. She bunched her fist and hit the shield in frustration, a tear rolling down her cheek as she continued to watch. This was *hell*.

Ryder recoiled as flames licked at his clothes. Gritting his teeth, he marshalled the flames, calling to the heat, to the light, drawing them into his palm until he balanced a flaming orb in his hand.

"Boys," Arthur said in low warning.

"I'm not walking away anymore, brother," Ryder snarled, emphasising the last word. "You need to face what you've done." He thrust the orb toward his brother, watching it envelop him. Hunter extinguished the flames, and Ryder took advantage of his distraction by running up and punching him in the face.

Hunter stumbled back, catching himself against the bookcase, then launched himself, grabbing Ryder around the chest and bringing him down. Ryder rolled, jabbing his brother in the jaw, blocking Hunter's attempt to grab his throat.

"You killed her," Ryder rasped as he straddled his brother.

Hunter's fist connected with his cheek, and Ryder fell to the side. Hunter rolled over him and grabbed his shirt, pulling his head off the floor. "I. Did. Not. Kill. Debbie." He stated, then punched him in the mouth. "You did."

Ryder coughed, tasting blood. He grabbed his brother's head and pressed his thumbs into his eye sockets, and Hunter roared as he jerked back. Ryder followed him over, his hands sliding in to pull at his brother's short hair. "I didn't."

Hunter glared. "You were home," he muttered.

"So were you," Ryder growled.

They froze there for a moment. Hunter frowned. "You didn't push her?"

Ryder's eyebrows dipped. "No. I thought you did."

Hunter shook his head, as much as Ryder would allow the movement. "No."

Ryder held up his finger in warning. "I swear, if you're lying to me ..."

"I'm not. I didn't kill her, I thought you did."

Both men turned to look at Arthur, and Vassi swallowed as he checked his manicure on one hand. "Took you long enough."

Hunter jackknifed to his feet, his expression shocked. Ryder was slower, his gaze wary.

"You were here, too."

Chapter Eighteen

Ryder tried to hide the shock washing over him. He'd learned never to reveal his true emotions to his father, but ... holy shit.

"Why?" Hunter rasped.

Arthur inclined his head toward Ryder. "Well, your brother started to piece it all together—of course, he was always a little quicker than you."

"What did you do?" Hunter growled, taking a step closer to the older man.

"Please. I merely gave you purpose."

Ryder's eyes narrowed in disbelief, in anger. "Purpose?"

Arthur nodded as he approached the fireplace, stretching his hands out as though to warm himself. "Of course. You boys have had it so easy," he murmured. "You have no idea what we light warriors have had to endure."

He turned to face them. "We were once a warrior race," he said, holding his hands out. "Now we're healers?" His expression showed his contempt. "Please. We should be the ruling class, here. We are stronger than all those miscreants," he sneered. "And yet we hide ourselves by making nice."

Hunter rolled his eyes. "Yes, Dad, we know. You miss those good old days." He lowered his head to glare at the man. "What does that have to do with us," he said, gesturing between Ryder and himself, "and Debbie?"

Arthur's lips lifted in a benevolent smile. "I've tried to teach you everything I know—and yet you're both content to just live your lives as *dentists*," he said scornfully. "I've built an empire, and you two are completely oblivious to your potential."

Ryder shook his head. "No, Dad. No we're not oblivious. We just didn't care." He stepped closer to his father, despite the fact that being this close to the man who sired him made his skin crawl. "Do you think I don't know what you're doing in that clinic of yours?" He shot his brother a glare. "What you're both doing?"

"At least Hunter shows ambition, Ryder. You—you were always so easygoing, so unassuming. You lacked drive, you lacked action. I gave you that with Debbie."

Hunter lifted a hand, a soft laugh of disbelief as he turned to Ryder. "Is he—" his jaw dropped, and he turned to the old man, "are you for real?"

"Tell me, son, did you hate your brother when you thought he killed your beloved?" Arthur hissed at Hunter. "Did you wrack your brain to find a way to make him pay? To make him hurt as much as he hurt you?" He turned his attention to Ryder. "And you? You left the family, finally took some action, showed some gumption, damn it."

Ryder's eyes widened as he shook his head. "I don't know you," he breathed. His own father ... "Debbie was a sweet girl, Dad. She didn't deserve to be treated like a pawn."

"Debbie was weak. A very malleable young lass—at least, until that last day. If she hadn't seen a witch about her blackouts ..." He sighed. "Damn witches." He waved a hand casually. "Anyway, it really was no trouble, suggesting she be sweet with you," Arthur stated, nodding at Ryder, then at Hunter, "and maybe a little spicy with you. You should be thanking me."

Ryder's eyebrows rose. "How the hell do you figure that?"

"Debbie was boring before I found her. I made her fun. For both of you." His father bowed. "You're welcome."

"You compelled her," Ryder said, shaking his head in disgust. He'd suspected, but having those suspicions confirmed made him sick to his stomach. "You manipulated her."

"What did you call her? The perfect woman? For both of you." Arthur nodded. "That's impressive work, if I do say so myself."

Hunter grabbed a book and threw it at his father. The book burst into a ball of flame and fell in a pile of ash to the floor before it could reach its target. Hunter ran at him, then cried out in pain, his knees buckling, as light arced from his father's fingers and around his head.

"No!" Ryder, fists clenched, ran at Arthur, only to stumble to a halt as white hot pain lanced through his brain. He clutched his head as he fell to his knees, gritting his teeth as his father's lightforce wrapped around him. His father was older, stronger, a light warrior prime who practised his dark skills on a daily basis. He tried to put up a mental shield, and his efforts muted the pain, but only slightly. As he writhed on the floor a movement at the window caught his eye. His eyes narrowed to see through the blinding pain, and he thought for a moment he was dreaming, as his father's lightforce leached into his mind.

Vassi.

Her pale face was pressed to the window, the sheen of tears glistening in the firelight. Her eyes glowed, her expression tight with fear, with horror. His beloved.

"Come ... in," he gasped, biting out the words.

Glass exploded as his half-blood vampire launched into the room, her fangs extended, her hair streaming behind her like a dark cloud of vengeance.

She moved in a blur, and then his father was on the floor, her teeth sinking into his throat.

The pain in Ryder's head fluttered, then disappeared, as Arthur Armstrong focused his attention on survival. Ryder rose to his feet as his father grabbed Vassi's arms. Her head reeled back and she screamed in pain as her skin started to burn where his father held her.

"No, damn it," he breathed, and flew at his dad.

His father moved fast, rolling over Vassi and bringing them both to their feet.

"Stop, or I'll kill—" his father growled in pain, then slid his hand down to grasp Vassi's wrist.

She whimpered as her skin sizzled under his touch, and he pulled her talons out from where she'd sunk them into his thigh. He lifted her hand up, and Ryder watched in horror as her talons flared into flame, falling to ash as she screamed in pain.

His brother's hand slapped on his arm, and Hunter used the grip to pull himself up. Ryder looked at his brother, who nodded. Individually, they couldn't take on the warrior prime. Together, they might stand a chance. As one, they turned to their father and summoned their lightforce. Arthur shoved Vassi to the floor, and she cried out in agony, nursing her badly burned hand as she tried to roll away.

Arthur smiled at them, the whites of his eyes visible, and he lifted both hands.

Sparks flew as each man threw out his power. Arthur created a wall of flame, an inferno that pushed back against the sons.

Ryder gritted his teeth at the searing heat. His father was older, and much, much more powerful. Sweat built up on his brow and lip as he felt the lightforce stutter under his father's onslaught. He tried to shore it up, and he knew Hunter was doing the same as they battled their light warrior prime.

Wind picked up in the room, but Ryder ignored it, focusing on pushing his lightforce back against his father. He tried to pierce the wall of flame with his own darts of light, hoping the little pricks of pain would distract his father enough for him and Hunter to vanquish him.

A noise teased at his focus, something that was at first a whisper, then grew into a chant, and finally a roar. Then he felt it. A lessening of force as the brunt of the flames diminished. A dampening spell.

His father frowned, then grimaced as he tried to build the wall up again, but something was pushing at it, something other than Ryder and his brother. It was slow-building and unrelenting, as the wind that had stirred up was suddenly sucked out of the room, his father's display of power along with it.

Ryder quickly glanced at Vassi lying injured on the floor, and rage rose within him. He doubled his efforts, channelling his lightforce as a blinding rope of lightning that snaked around his father, and he hurled a blast that knocked his father clear off his feet and against the bookcase with such force the whole structure collapsed and their father appeared to be embedded in the plaster, his head cracking against the wall with a loud thunk. Arthur hung there, unconscious, until Ryder drew in his talent. He didn't bother to watch his father fall to the floor, his attention on the woman who'd saved him.

"Nice work. Who the hell is that?" Hunter asked, frowning. "And what just happened?"

"She's a vamp. And she's my lawyer." She was so much more than that, but he wasn't about to explain that to his brother, not yet. There were still some things that needed to be cleared up, namely Jared Gray's murder. He decided not to mention the witches he was sure had accompanied Vassi.

"She's cute."

"She's mine."

Hunter held up his hands. "Don't worry, brother. I learn my lessons." He rose to his feet, and grimaced as he pulled at his singed shirtfront. "This was my favourite shirt."

Ryder knelt by her side and gently brushed the dark hair off her face. "Vassi," he whispered. Her eyes fluttered open, shimmering with tears. "It's okay, sweetheart. It's going to be fine."

"Let me see," Hunter said brusquely and reached for her hand. Ryder grabbed his brother's wrist, preventing his brother from touching his mate. Hunter arched an eyebrow.

"I won't hurt her, Ryder. I can help her." His brother smiled. "I wouldn't hurt your mate."

He didn't kill Debbie. Ryder had to force himself to remember that. It was so hard to let go of all that anger, all that resentment, all that hate. But Hunter was an adept, able to heal across disciplines. If Vassi had injured her fangs, Ryder was the one to help. Unfortunately he wasn't a surgeon—but Hunter was. He reluctantly let go of his brother. Hunter lifted her hand gently, and Ryder cringed, both at the hiss of her breath, and the damage he could see to her fingers. "She injured one of them before," he said quietly. When she'd had to defend herself against the werewolves. Despair swept through him. He'd caused her so much trouble, so much damn pain.

Hunter nodded, and Vassi gasped, trying to pull her hand back as he turned it over gently. "I just need to see," he told her in a voice that surprised Ryder with its warm compassion. Vassi stared at him warily.

Ryder looked at his brother, then at the woman who held his heart. "Trust him," he said softly. Hunter glanced at him, blinked and looked back down at her injuries. He closed his eyes, and Ryder watched as tendrils of light stretched from his brother's hand, spreading out to gently caress Vassi's charred skin. He appreciated the care his brother took, sensing the tenderness he wielded as the lightforce slid under her skin. Vassi's eyes widened as the burns slowly disappeared from her hand, her skin returning to a healthy pink. She winced, just a little, as the stubs of the talons slowly edged out from underneath her nails. It took several minutes, but then Hunter covered her hand with his, his eyes opening. He winked at Vassi's expression of surprise.

"I know you can self-heal, but I'm faster. I've taken away the pain," he told Ryder. "The talons are gone on this hand. She'll need an operation to replace them, but she's fine until then."

Vassi sat up, and Ryder leaned down to kiss her hungrily, his relief at her recovery quickly turning to something hotter as she returned his kiss.

Then Hunter cleared his throat. "Ah, don't mind me. I just live here."

Ryder pulled back, regretfully, but smiled at Vassi. Her cheeks were pink, and her teeth flashed in a smile, but he could still see some shadows in her eyes.

She'd heard, he realised. She knew about Debbie.

And yet she'd still flown through that window like an avenging angel. God he loved this woman.

"Thank you," he murmured. She wasn't supposed to get hurt. He'd tried to leave her, tried to protect her, but she'd followed him. "I thought I fired you."

"You did, but seeing as I didn't take any notice of you the first couple of times you did it, I thought why bother now?" She arched an eyebrow.

Hunter chuckled. "Oh, the vamp has sass."

Arthur Armstrong stirred, and Vassi reached out with her other hand, a talon sliding out as she scratched the man along the neck. A scarlet trail of blood seeped over the collar of his snow white tux. He moaned.

Hunter frowned. "Whoa. And claws."

"Blood loss will weaken him. Don't worry, it's not fatal, but I don't want anymore lightning shows until we can properly restrain him."

"Good point. I'll go get the irons." Hunter rose from the floor and walked from the room.

"Irons?" Vassi looked up at him in enquiry.

Ryder nodded. She was being professional, and despite their kiss, just a little distant. She was hurt.

"Yeah. Silver binds vampires and werewolves. Iron binds a light warrior."

Hunter returned. He was wearing gloves, and he worked quickly to attach the manacles to his father's wrists and ankles.

Even from here, Ryder could hear the sting as the metal touched the man's skin, and felt no regret.

Vassi rose to her feet, her legs long and sexy in those tight jeans he liked to see her in. Then again, he liked to see her out of them, too. She folded her arms, and he frowned, again sensing the distance between them.

"So, who killed Jared Gray?"

Chapter Nineteen

"He did."

Vassi arched an eyebrow as each brother pointed to the other. The men looked at each other in surprise. Great. She inhaled, then exhaled slowly, expanding her awareness and letting her gift rise.

Hunter put his hands on his hips. "You think I killed an alpha prime?"

Ryder frowned. "It reeks of you. Unlike me, you use wolfsbane in your surgery. You blew up the apothecary, and your morals are questionable."

Hunter grimaced. "I may have killed a witch, too." He sighed. "I feel bad about that, actually. You know me, though. It's such a struggle being good when being bad feels *so* good."

Vassi blinked. Hunter's feedback was warm. He actually regretted what he'd done at the apothecary, despite his effort at levity. She looked toward the doorway. Dave and Melissa were still MIA, although she knew they were responsible for the flame vacuum. She could scarcely believe it had taken two light warriors and two witches to knock out a warrior prime. For some reason, though, the witches had decided to remain hidden. After what Hunter had done to Ryder, she wasn't going to alleviate his conscience.

"But I didn't kill the wolf." He shrugged. "Why would I?"

Vassi's eyes narrowed. Again, she sensed warmth. She didn't understand. She was so sure Hunter was responsible for this whole mess.

"Woodland Pack was fed instructions to deliver the tainted supplies to my clinic. I know they come to your clinic for treatment. I know you can compel, and I saw Rafe Woodland's teeth. The work he's had done would cost far more than they can afford, with all the territorial squabbles they have going on." Ryder glared at his brother.

Vassi turned her attention to Hunter, who held up a finger. "I don't compel," he said. "I dreamwalk. There is a difference."

"And you put people to sleep in your clinic," Ryder pointed out. "Plenty of opportunity to tip-toe through those dreams and plant suggestions." He waved his fingers.

Hunter arched an eyebrow. "I don't tip-toe through dreams," he said. "I drift. But I didn't drift through Rafe Woodland's dreams." He shuddered. "Rafe Woodland is not my patient."

There. A tendril of cool deceit.

"What do you know, Hunter?" she asked coolly. Perhaps it was time to try different questions. She stretched her gift out, teasing at his mind. Damn it, she wished she had her lipstick.

Hunter eyed her suspiciously. "I know you're a strange one."

She smiled. "If Rafe Woodland wasn't your patient, whose was he?"

Hunter nodded. "My father's."

Vassi nodded at the warm sensation that went with that answer. "So while Rafe Woodland was a patient at the clinic, he came and saw your father, not you?"

Hunter dipped his head. "Correct."

Ryder frowned. "Then why attack the witch? Why destroy her apothecary?"

Hunter gave a mock cringe. "This is embarrassing," he said, then sighed. "I did it for you, bro."

Vassi's eyebrows rose. Wow. Ryder's brother was ... wow. She eyed the man she couldn't stop thinking about, couldn't stop this huge tide of emotion that welled up inside her at the mere sight of him. Apparently she'd fallen in love with the only sane member of the family. Thank God.

Ryder's face showed perfect confusion. "I don't follow."

Hunter leaned against the desk. "You said it yourself. I already have my supply of wolfsbane, and I know you don't normally use the stuff. When Gray's autopsy reports came out—"

"How did you get the autopsy reports?" Vassi asked. "They haven't been released to the public yet."

Hunter rolled his eyes. "Like I'm actually going to wait for that to happen." He shrugged. "I know people who know people. Let's just leave it at that."

Vassi pursed her lips as she motioned for him to continue.

"So, I figured you had to order the wolfsbane from somewhere, and it wasn't hard to find the one supplier in town who could give you that highly concentrated form of the poison. So I paid her a visit."

"You destroyed her business," Ryder exclaimed. "Why?"

Hunter scowled. "She was peddling poisons to anyone who would pay for them. At least when I administer it, I monitor it. She hands it over willy-nilly. Do you have any idea how many patients come into my clinic from accidental or intended poisoning? She sells it to a housewife one day, whose werewolf husband winds up in my surgery the next. She might think she's doing a service, but she's basically putting a loaded gun into the hands of her customers."

Ryder folded his arms, his look expectant.

"Fine, and maybe I thought if I destroyed any record of you purchasing the poison, then perhaps your fancy-pants lawyer here could get you acquitted."

Vassi's jaw dropped at the warmth that washed over her. "Good grief, you're telling the truth."

Hunter's eyes narrowed as he gazed at her with a new wariness. "Of course I'm telling the truth."

She glanced at Ryder. His expression was just as shocked. Then he held up a hand as he tried to take a calming breath. "You do realise that you destroyed any evidence that could prove my innocence?"

Hunter grimaced. "Oops. My bad."

Vassi watched Ryder as he stalked away a short distance, shaking his head and muttering. She put her hands on her hips and looked down at her toes, her thoughts racing. "Okay," she said quietly. She looked at Ryder, his expression stony. "I know you're not guilty of killing Jared Gray," she said, then turned to Hunter, "And you're guilty of stupidity and protecting your younger brother—" she hesitated. An over-inflated sense of protection seemed to run in the family. "So if neither of you actually killed Jared Gray, who did? Who stands to gain if Ryder goes to prison?"

Ryder frowned. "If convicted of murder, I'd be stripped of my assets," he said. "So Hunter would get my share of this house as part of an inheritance from my mother, along with the rest of my trust fund ..."

"Trust fund?" Vassi frowned. "Why am I only just hearing about this now?"

Ryder gestured to Hunter. "Our mother was wealthy in her own right. We each have a trust fund that matures when we both reach thirty."

"Well, you're nearly twenty-eight," Vassi said. She remembered reading it in her file. She turned to Hunter. "When do you turn thirty?"

"Next month."

"Who is the executor?"

Both men looked down at the man at their feet. Arthur opened his eyes to slits.

"This is so painful, listening to you all muddle your way through this," he muttered. "Kill me now."

Vassi crossed over to him and hunkered down on her heels. "Did you kill Jared Gray?"

His eyes widened for a moment. "No."

Cold, bone-chilling, mind-numbing cold.

She looked up at Ryder. "He's lying."

Ryder chewed his cheek, slowly nodding. "I see."

"I don't," Hunter said. "I really don't."

"Well, if I had my lipstick ..." she said meaningfully.

Ryder shook his head. "No. Not with my dad. No way in hell." He shuddered, then shook his hands and arms as though someone had walked over his grave. "Ugh."

"Explain this to me. Dad killed Gray. Why?" Hunter folded his arms across his chest.

"How did you finance your clinic?" she asked Ryder, and he closed his eyes as realisation hit.

"I borrowed against my trust fund, with a caveat. The loan has an automatic overriding draw once the fund matures. Any outstanding debts are paid before the rest of the fund is awarded to me."

"So you were already chipping away at the money."

"But I'm older. Why didn't he try to kill me?" Hunter asked, half-curious, half-petulant.

"Are you seriously upset that he didn't try to destroy your life first?" Ryder asked in exasperation.

"You're right. There are times when being the favoured son sucks. I should enjoy this moment."

"Have you touched your trust fund?" she asked Hunter, and he shook his head.

"See, he had another month to worry about you. Your brother, on the other hand, was already spending his inheritance. If Ryder died, all the money would go to you, and he had another month to organise your death, thus receiving both funds. Do you have your own will?"

Hunter closed his eyes briefly as he shook his head, then opened them to stare at his father. "You'd be my only living relative. Did you plan to kill me, too, old man?"

"No," Arthur grunted from the floor. "It's not true, boys, don't listen to her." He opened his eyes and tried to sit up, hissing as the iron cuffs singed his skin.

Vassi shivered at the arctic blast when she met the man's narrowed gaze. "He's lying."

"So he manipulated his patient to murder an enemy pack leader and make it look like I did it. If I went to jail, he'd get my inheritance. If the lycans managed to kill me before my trial, he'd get my inheritance."

Hunter gazed down at his father. "That is seriously fucked up."

"And thinking each of you was guilty of murder not once, but twice, isn't?" Vassi asked pointedly. Both brothers looked at each other sheepishly. She shook her head and stalked over to what looked like a phone cord. She lifted it, following the trail around splintered furniture until she found the phone.

"I'm calling the police. They can take him in."

Hunter hunkered down to meet his father's eyes. "You are no longer my father. I am no longer your son. Like Ryder, I'm taking Mother's name." He smiled, baring his teeth. "So your family, the one you wanted to be strong and rule your precious empire? It no longer exists. The Armstrong name dies with you."

Arthur squeezed his eyes closed as Hunter stood up. "Seriously fucked up," Hunter muttered. He turned to Vassi. "You're going to trust the Reform Court with him?" He shook his head. "He'll lie, he'll compel, he'll weasel his sorry arse out of jail."

Vassi smiled as she dialled the local police number. "They'll take the appropriate measures, and I'm sure a truthseeker can sort out fact from fiction. I happen to know a good one."

"Ehhh," Hunter said, sounding like a game show buzzer. "Conflict of interest. Bond mates can't represent each other in court," he said gesturing between her and Ryder.

She frowned, as did Ryder.

"You know she's a truthseeker?"

"What do you mean, bond mate?"

Hunter smiled as he pointed to Ryder. "Uh, it was fairly obvious, the way her eyes go all black when she says liar," he replied, deepening his voice for dramatic effect on the last word. He then turned to Vassi, his eyes widening as his gaze darted back and forth between the two. "You didn't tell her? Hell, the link is so fresh and sparkly, it's damn near blinding," he said, then gave a throaty chuckle. "Oh. Wow. You two have a lot to talk about." He clasped his hands together. "Well, this is awkward." He grimaced, then gestured over his shoulder. "I'll uh—um," he tapped his watch. "I need to be … somewhere else," he whispered, then backed towards the door.

Ryder glared at his retreating brother. "Do you want the good news or the bad news?"

"Give me the good news, brother. I think I need it, right about now."

"The good news is that the witch survived. The bad news is—the witch survived." Ryder shook his head. "What the hell were you thinking?"

Vassi watched as Dave and Melissa stepped into the room, each placing a hand on Hunter's shoulders. Hunter's eyes rolled back and he sagged, unconscious. Dave caught him, then hoisted him over his shoulder.

"Damn witches," Arthur spat out.

"Don't hurt him," Ryder called out, stepping toward them.

Melissa turned and eyed him for a moment, her expression solemn. "He almost killed me. Tribal law says almost killing him is a fair response."

"He's a douche, but he's not evil. I can't let you hurt him."

Melissa's eyes darkened with anger. "And I can't let him get away with what he did to me. He needs to be punished. Consider this me calling in that I.O.U."

Ryder ran his hand through his hair in frustration, and Vassi could sense his dilemma. A man of integrity, he had to honour his debt, but this request would rub against his protective instincts. His honour finally won out, and he reluctantly nodded.

The witches left as Vassi quietly murmured instructions over the phone. She kept her eye on Ryder, who now looked around the room, resigned to the decimation of his home, of his family.

When she received reassurance that the necessary authorities were on their way, she disconnected the call and folded her arms.

He walked over to her, his hips swaying in that sexy way of his, his blue stare intense. He detoured via his belligerent father, and his fist shot out so fast it was almost a blur as it connected with the older man's chin. Arthur's head snapped around, and he slumped to the floor, unconscious. Again.

"Yeah, that feels better," he muttered, shaking out his hand.

He cocked his head, then stepped closer to her. He rubbed her arms. "We need to talk."

* * *

Hours later, they sat in the reception parlour. Ryder sat on the sofa opposite Vassi. She'd insisted on sitting across from him, the fire roaring in the great hearth. The police had left, dragging a still-unconscious Arthur Armstrong out to a prison van. Ryder made sure to brief them on the proper handling of his father, without having to tell them exactly what he was. He may have cut ties with his father, but he was still a light warrior. Secrecy on that subject was drilled into him from birth, and not quite so easy to shed. One slip, though, and Hunter was right, his father would weasel his sorry arse out of prison.

He leaned back in the sofa, a glass tumbler of scotch in his hand. Vassi had accepted his offer of one, but had yet to take a sip. He sighed. Her legs were crossed, her arms folded, her expression remote.

"I'm sorry," he began.

She arched an eyebrow. "For what? For firing me in some transparent move to keep me out of trouble because you don't trust me? For not mentioning that you happened to love some paragon of virtue who is so high on a pedestal she may as well be a saint? Or for this bond mate thing? What is that, by the way?"

He slid off the lounge and knelt at her feet. "I'm so sorry, for all of that."

"Fine. Consider all forgiven. I'm going home, because once the news report breaks, lycans won't be stalking my home." She made to get up, but he put his hand on her knee, forestalling her.

"You have every right to be angry," he said quietly. "And I know you're hurt. Please, let me explain."

She met his gaze, then subsided back against the sofa. "You have two minutes."

"Okay, let me start with your employment. I did it for your protection." He held up a hand when she opened her mouth. "I know, you didn't like it, but if it came down to keeping you out of danger, I would happily fire you again. In a heartbeat."

Her eyes flared, and he took a breath. Paused. How could he make her understand? He'd never talked about what had happened, had never had to define it—and certainly hadn't discussed it with his family until tonight. That he was ready, willing and wanting to do so with Vassi told him there had been a monumental shift in his emotions.

"I once had a girlfriend," he began. "Her name was Debbie. She died, Vassi. Dead. Gone. Final. This was a dangerous situation." He hesitated, struggling to find the right words. "I couldn't keep Debbie safe, I couldn't protect her—from my own family, for Pete's sake." The memory of Debbie lying on the pavement, her last breath escaping as the light in her eyes died … the image flickered, and in his mind's eye it was Vassi he saw dying on the driveway. The emotion that image brought forth was almost crippling, and far more devastating. He cupped her face. "When Debbie died, it hurt so damn much. I walked away from my family, from the business. If *you* died—" he looked into her eyes, saw the beauty, the caring, the life—all that could have been gone in a heartbeat. "All that hurt would not compare to my devastation if I got you killed. Do you understand?" He bit his lip for a moment, then pulled her hand to cover his chest.

"You are everything to me. Any breath without you is too painful. My thoughts, my actions, my heart—they're all yours. I will do whatever it takes to keep you safe."

She swallowed. "Keep talking."

He nodded, hustling a little closer to her on the floor. She uncrossed her legs and he put both hands on her thighs.

"As you heard, Debbie was a woman both I and Hunter … knew."

"And loved," she whispered.

He cocked his head, then shook it slowly as he thought about it. "Not quite. We each loved who we thought she was. When she died, I had my suspicions that perhaps my father had something to do with how I responded to her, and how Hunter responded to her. I loved a fake." He shrugged. "I loved a woman who didn't exist. And then I thought my brother killed her."

Vassi's gaze softened, and she ran her hand through his hair. "From someone who doesn't have one, trust me—family is important," she whispered.

His eyebrows rose. "My father killed my girlfriend, tried to have me killed, and would have killed my brother. Hunter thought I'd killed everyone I thought he killed. He blew up a witch's store, nearly killing said witch in the process. Sometimes it's good to be on your own."

She smiled. "So your family isn't perfect. I'm totally fine with you walking away from your father, but what you and your brother have—it's still salvageable. You have to remember, despite all this time hating him—your brother didn't kill Debbie. He didn't kill Jared, either, and although he did annihilate Melissa's store, he did it to help you. Tonight, you two worked well together."

Ryder frowned. "Well, it might be a moot point. Melissa has him now, and something tells me she's not going to let bygones be bygones." He shook his head. "I know I owe her, but I can't just let her kill my brother."

"Don't worry, Dave won't let her break tribal law—their mother wouldn't approve. Hunter will be back when Melissa decides he's been punished enough." She arched an eyebrow. "Now tell me about this bond mate business."

He gently pushed her thighs apart, and kneeled between them. "It's rare. Light warriors have no control over it. A few can actually see it, like my brother. I can't." He raised his hands to cup her face. "It's when two people share such deep, honest emotion that they also share a consciousness," he whispered, then kissed her cheek. "When their hearts and minds are bound as one," he said, turning her head so he could kiss her neck. He felt her shudder in his arms, and need, hot and obsessive, raced through him. "When they share a great love." He trailed his lips down her throat, felt her pulse jump beneath his caress.

She pulled his head back to look him in the eye. "We share a great love? We've only known each other for a short while—and didn't you think you shared a great love with Debbie?"

He read the doubt, the insecurity, the pain in her eyes, and felt true regret at causing it. "I knew my father my whole life and I never realised how evil he could be, how he could easily discard me and my brother for our mother's money." He smiled sadly. "I've seen so much of your character over the last few days—you took my case, even though you didn't really want to. You defended me when you thought I could be a killer, and you risked your life to find out the truth. We've shared so much more in the last few days than many people get to share in a lifetime."

He delved into his pocket and withdrew a familiar tube. She gasped, her eyes widening. He removed the lid, rotated the base, and handed her the scarlet lipstick. "Now, ask me again how I feel about you."

She kept her gaze on his as she applied the coating to her lips, the rich colour sliding on with ease. Then she pressed her lips together, ever so gently in a slow, erotic smack. His body clenched with need, and then she lowered her lips to his.

He drew her in, his arms sliding around her back, his tongue rubbing, duelling against hers, as a sensual fog filled his mind. She pulled back.

"Do you have any feelings for Debbie?" she asked, her eyes narrowed.

"Regret. Sadness. Tenderness." He rattled off the words as they sprang to his mind. It felt like she was reaching in to draw out that secret part of him he'd kept hidden for so long, and he had no control over what she revealed.

"Do you love me?" she whispered.

"With all my heart," he answered without thinking. He looked at her solemnly. "I would go to war for you." He'd thought that when she'd told him in the car about her lack of family. Now, he was her family. She caught her lip between her teeth, her eyes shimmering with unshed tears. She understood the reference, believed his vow.

He leaned forward, and she trembled when his chest rubbed against her breasts. "Let me show you how much I love you," he whispered, as he took her lips in a long, drugging kiss.

Chapter Twenty

Vassi moaned as she leaned back against the plump sofa cushions, Ryder's lips were driving her crazy with hot need as he kissed his way down to her collarbone. He made a noise of frustration, then his hands were tugging her shirt out of her jeans, and up over her head.

"Oh, God, I've been fantasising about your breasts all night." He covered them with his palms, and she shuddered at the warm caress as he lifted a nipple to his lips. He sucked her into his mouth, as though she satisfied a gut-wrenching craving.

Then she felt it, the awareness, as though a connection within her flared to life, stretching toward him. His sensations, the weight of her breasts in his hands, him stroking her nipple with his tongue, she could feel everything he felt, layered within her own sensations. Desire rippled through him, through her, building into a sweet torturous hunger.

She arched her back, crying out as the rhythmic suck and tug on her breasts sent an answering sensation down to her cervix. She wrapped her legs around his waist, drawing him in tighter to her body. She could feel his ridged arousal throbbing against her, could feel the blood pounding to his cock, his need for her, her need for him. It was confusing, delightful. Wicked. Her hands delved into his dark hair, tugging on the strands until he released her breast with a pop. She pulled his head up to her, kissing him with an abandon that she knew he could feel, and sensed it feeding his own passion for her.

His hands dropped to her waist, tugging at the opening to her jeans, then fumbling behind him to pull off her boots, sending them flying in different directions. His stare hot and heavy with intent, he maintained eye contact as he lifted her hips and yanked at her jeans and underwear, her breasts bobbing with the jerking movement. He stripped her, quickly and efficiently, his aim to get her naked as quickly as possible.

Then he rose, his hands pulling at his own clothes with a powerful urgency. She stood as he kicked off his jeans, then gasped as he lifted her, clasping her thighs around his waist. He took a couple of steps, backing her up against the dark wood panelling next to the fireplace. She moaned as he pressed her against the solid wall, the cool timber against her back, his hot chest rubbing against her breasts. She caressed him, her arms around his shoulders, loving the feel of the muscles moving there as he held her in place.

"I need you," he groaned. "Now."

"Do it," she whispered, then tilted her head back against the wall as he slid inside her, her desire already making her slick for his entry. He filled her, his length impaling her as she opened herself up to him. She clenched around him, moaning as he slowly withdrew, then lunged inside again. She could feel him, not just inside her, but inside *him*. She knew the intense pleasure, the excruciating delight at her embrace, as he fed her those sensations.

He thrust into her, again and again, holding her up as tension tightened within her, hot need eating away at her control. She bucked her hips to meet his thrusts, and he lowered his head to again latch onto a nipple. She cried out at the fierce constriction of hunger, the ratcheting eagerness to climb that peak, until finally she reached the top, plunging into the abyss of pleasure—hers, his, theirs.

They cried out in unison at their mutual release, frozen for a moment, before breath finally returned.

Panting, Ryder pressed his lips to hers. "I love you," he whispered.

"I believe you," she said, then wrapped her arms around his neck. "I love you, too."

* * *

"So in light of the findings, Your Honour, the people would like to drop the charges against Ryder Galen," Taylor Henley stated calmly.

Vassi kept the emotion out of her expression, presenting a serene front to the packed courtroom.

Judge Flack nodded. "The murder charges against Ryder Galen are dropped." She glanced at Ryder, standing next to Vassi. "The case is dismissed, you are free to go." She banged her gavel.

"We also request a charge of conspiracy to murder be brought against Arthur Armstrong, Your Honour. Due to his access to funds, we ask he be held without bail in a secure institution as he awaits trial."

The judge nodded. "So be it. Arthur Armstrong will stand trial for conspiracy to murder Alpha Prime Jared Gray, along with Rafe Woodland, Alpha Prime of Woodland Pack. An arrest warrant shall be issued for Mr. Woodland. Meanwhile Woodland Pack will make restitution for Mr Galen's vehicle. Sanctions will be instituted against the pack for their actions against a protected court officer."

Vassi's gaze met Ryder's smirk. They'd already talked about his new car. He wanted another bloody hatchback, Blanche II.

"Excuse me, Your Honour," Taylor interrupted before she could hit her gavel again. "We have a request for jurisdiction transfer."

The judge raised her eyebrows, but nodded. "I'll hear it."

Taylor turned and beckoned to the back of the room. Vassi turned out of curiosity, then hid her surprise as a familiar figure made his way to the front.

Matthias nodded at her briefly as he swung open the gate that led to the trial area. "Your honour, my name is Matthias Marshall, Guardian Prime and nominated representative of Alpine Pack. Our Acting Alpha Prime, Samantha Alpine, formally requests that Rafe Woodland's charges be transferred under tribal jurisdiction to the Alpine Pack."

The judge inclined her head. "Request granted." She hit her gavel with a resounding crack, then nodded with satisfaction. She gestured to the bailiff, who stepped forward.

"All rise," he intoned, and the crowd within the courtroom stood. As soon as the judge had left the room, the noise erupted. Vassi flung her arms around Ryder's neck as he chuckled warmly.

"Thank you," he whispered to her, and she squeezed him tighter.

"You're welcome."

Someone cleared a throat behind them, and she turned. Taylor.

He smiled at her, his brown eyes warm. "Good work, counsellor." He stuck his hand out and she accepted the gesture, grinning. "You've cleared my trial schedule for this week. Thanks." Then he winked. "See you next time."

He leaned over to grab his briefcase, nodded at Ryder, then walked through the swing gate and into the crowd.

"Come on, let's get out of here," she said to Ryder, then halted as Matthias blocked their way. She felt Ryder stiffen next to her.

Ryder lifted his chin. "I'm sorry about what happened to your alpha."

Matthias nodded slowly. "We understand it was unintentional," he said quietly. "We'll be going after those truly responsible."

"Rafe Woodland won't be easy to bring down," Ryder commented. "I'd like to help." He glanced at Vassi. "He tried to harm my family."

Warmth bloomed within her at his words. It was so weird, so ... new, having someone who wanted to look out for her, protect her, defend her. It was an alien sensation, but one she looked forward to getting accustomed to.

Matthias smiled. "We like a challenging hunt," he said, then inclined his head. "Thank you, we'll keep your offer in mind." He turned to Vassi and nodded. "Vamp."

Ryder put his arm around Vassi's shoulders in a clear display of territory to the lycan. Matthias's smile broadened and he winked at Vassi, then turned to leave the courtroom, a large number of lycans following in his wake. Each of them nodded solemnly at Ryder as they left.

"He'd make a good alpha," Ryder commented, then grimaced. "As long as he stays out of Irondell."

Vassi nodded. "He would, but not for Alpine. He needs to find his own pack."

"Speaking of pack, and family, I don't suppose you've heard anything from Dave yet about my brother? I'm thinking of launching a search party."

Vassi shook her head. "I haven't heard from either of them."

"Should I be worried?"

"No. Hunter should be, though. Melissa can be quite the bitch."

Ryder sighed as he started to walk with her out of the courtroom. "I guess he deserves it. I saw what he did. She's lucky to be alive."

"I think they kind of deserve each other," she whispered, then smiled as Ryder chuckled.

"Let's go home," Ryder murmured, steering her toward the elevators.

"Vassi—wait!"

Vassi turned at the familiar voice. Seraphina hurried toward her, oblivious to the stares and gawks she left in her wake. The gorgeous cambion exuded a sexy, carefree air, effortlessly enchanting those she passed. She halted in front of them, her blonde hair cascading in a tumble of curls to her shoulders, blue eyes sparkling.

Seraphina's eyes widened when she noticed Ryder, her smile changing from friendly to seductive in the blink of an eye. "Oh, hello gorgeous." She touched him on his suit sleeve. "You are even sexier in the flesh." She looked at Vassi. "Tell me your volcanic snatch is getting a workout."

Honestly, there were some things only Seraphina could get away with. Vassi winced. "If your snatch feels 'volcanic', you need a healer, not a lover," she said tartly. "And it's none of your business, either way."

Seraphina waved her two fists in a muted cheer. "Yay! Vassi finally got laid."

Vassi closed her eyes briefly, ignoring Ryder's shocked laugh, then assumed her serene courtroom look. "Why are you here, Sera, and not back at the office?"

Seraphina's eyes widened. "Oh, you are not going to believe this. Vivianne Marchetta requested a meeting. Now."

Vassi's eyebrows rose, then she gulped as the woman herself approached. With long brown hair, dark brown eyes and a knowing smile, she looked like seduction personified and next to Seraphina that was a hard look to pull off.

Vivianne smiled, her hands rising to rest on her hips, as she slowly walked around Vassi, eyeing her up and down.

"So this is the half-blood who caused a werewolf pack to enter my territory," she mused.

Vassi grimaced, and Ryder squeezed her hand in encouragement. "Uh, about that—" she began but halted as the woman waved her hand carelessly.

"Oh, don't worry about that. Tribal law dictates that I can retaliate—and I do so love to retaliate," she said, her lips lifting in a smile that was both beautiful and dangerous. "I wanted to see the lawyer who risked her life for her client." She eyed Ryder, then nodded, "I can see why."

She faced Vassi, folding her arms across her chest, and arched an eyebrow. "You didn't get paid for this case, did you?"

Vassi shook her head. "No, it was part of our pro-bono requirement."

"So you took on not one, but two werewolf packs, as well as a crime boss," she observed. "I like that. I want you to work for me."

Vassi frowned. "I already do work for you. I work for Campbell, Singh & Partners," she said, confused. "You have my firm on retainer."

Vivianne smiled. "Ah, but I want you to work for just me." She tilted her head. "You may not realise it, but Arthur Armstrong has been like an annoying rat in my pantry for a number of years." Her gaze darted at Ryder. "No offence."

His eyes narrowed.

"With Armstrong looking drab in prison orange, I suddenly have a world of opportunity in front of me, and I have a little motto—any enemy of my enemy is my friend. I'm in the market for a special kind of lawyer." Her eyes narrowed. "Your kind."

"You mean the kind who respects the law and upholds it?" Vassi wanted to clarify any expectation. She knew Marchetta's business—both Vivianne and her brother Lucien straddled the grey area between legal and downright illicit, and Vassi wanted the woman to understand which side of that line she stood on.

Vivianne nodded. "We understand each other perfectly." She withdrew a metal case from her handbag and snapped it open to withdraw a business card. "Think about it, then call me."

"Her assistant goes with her," Seraphina interjected quickly, then mirrored the frown Vassi shot at her. "You are not going to leave me alone with RB."

Vivianne eyed the cambion with curiosity, then shrugged. "Fine." She adjusted the strap of her handbag on her arm and gave Vassi one last look. "Call me."

The woman strode away, her hips swaying in the short black skirt as men stopped to let her through.

Seraphina clapped her hands. "Oh. My. GAWD. We are moving up in the world, Vassi."

"I haven't made up my mind, Sera," Vassi reminded her assistant. Sera rolled her eyes.

"Please. It's a great opportunity to expand your legal experience, much faster than at Campbell, Singh & Partners. Besides, her executives are H.O.T."

Vassi glanced at Ryder, shocked at what had just transpired. His eyebrows rose, then he shrugged. "Whatever you decide, I'll support."

"Even if she's your father's enemy?"

"Well, that's a growing group. You heard her—an enemy of her enemy is her friend. I'd say that qualifies us as the best of buddies, wouldn't you?"

"I'm going to clean out my desk. I can't wait for Lara Dyson to catch wind of this," Seraphina said.

"I still haven't decided, Sera," Vassi said.

Seraphina nodded as she started to back away. "I understand. You think about it. When you've made your decision, call me. I'll be the one cleaning out both our desks." The cambion skipped away, looking almost like a sexy executive sprite in her office clothes and bouncing curls.

Ryder shook his head. "That's a lot of energy. Where is she going?"

"She's happy. She'll want to enjoy the buzz and look for someone to … share it with her," she said meaningfully, and Ryder nodded.

"I see."

She pressed the button for the elevator, then folded her arms. "So, I've just had an amazing job offer. What does the future hold for you, Mr. Galen?"

He grimaced. "Well, with Arthur in prison and Hunter in witchy-woo hell, someone's got to run the clinics. There are patients who still need treatment. When Hunter returns, we'll make some decisions then."

The door slid open and they stepped inside the elevator. Ryder held up a hand and shook his head as another lawyer attempted to enter the lift. "We're full," he said, and pressed the button to close the doors.

Vassi arched a brow as Ryder backed her up against the wall. "I have been wanting to get you alone since we got out of bed this morning," he murmured, his voice low and deep.

She swallowed as he gazed down at her, his eyes hot with arousal.

"I want to strip these clothes off your body and kiss you all over," he whispered against her neck, his warm breath causing her to tremble. "I want to make love to you in this elevator while everyone waiting for it wonders why it's taking so long, then realises exactly what we were doing when we get out—and wish they could do the same."

He slid a finger under the hem of her short skirt, caressing her thigh. "I want to be inside you and have you scream my name so the whole building knows you're mine. And I'm yours."

Her teeth caught her lip, and her hand shot out to press the red stop button on the panel. The elevator jolted to a stop. An alarm started to ring.

"Then do it," she said, and was rewarded with a wicked smile and a flare of heat in his gaze.

"God, I hate you," he whispered as he kissed her neck. She gasped at the cold tendril that teased at her, and she laughed.

"Liar."

Acknowledgments

I would like to thank the following inspirations who contributed to this story:

Rudi Bremer, Euge, Kat Mayo, Allison Rogers, @SlightlySammi, Vivianne. Your ideas were amazing—and sometimes downright disturbing, but always awesome. To the TWC Press Team: Jennifer Brassel, Donna Gallagher, Coleen Kwan, Maggie Nash, Paula Roe, Deborah Tait—thank you all for your amazing generosity in the production of this story.

A very special thank you to the Better Read Than Dead bookstore for being the birthplace of this novel, and giving us the time and space to 'what if'. You earned your place in our story!

And thanks to Mad E Pizza for the limoncello shots—you made the bizarre sound increasingly logical in our plot-storming.

Oh—and thank you Sarah from Smart Bitches for teaching us not to take ourselves too seriously, as well as sharing a love for romance—and some incredible euphemisms!

About the author

Shannon Curtis has worked as a copywriter, business consultant, admin manager, customer service rep, logistics co-ordinator, dangerous goods handler, event planner, switch bitch and betting agent. She decided to try writing a story like those she loved to read when she found herself at home after the birth of her first child. Her books have been finalists for Favourite Romantic Suspense for 2011, 2012 and 2013, as well as Favourite Continuing Romance Series as voted by the Australian Romance Readers Association, and she was selected to write romance novels for *The Bold and The Beautiful* series. She loves reading, loves writing, and loves hearing from her readers, so visit her at www.shannoncurtis.com and say hi!

Follow her on Twitter: @2BShannonCurtis

Find her on Facebook:
https://www.facebook.com/Shannon.Curtis.Writers.Ink

Visit her website: www.shannoncurtis.com

Visit her blog: http://shannoncurtis.wordpress.com/

About the publishers

Australian Romance Readers Association

The Australian Romance Readers Association started in 2007 after a chance remark in an online forum; *'maybe we should have our own romance readers convention'* was met with an overwhelming response. From an original membership of sixteen, that number has swelled and is constantly growing. With an online blog, monthly newsletter and regular reader events, along with an annual awards ceremony recognising excellence in romance fiction and a biennial romance readers' convention, the Australian Romance Readers Association is the home and heart of romance for readers.

ARRA's goal is to:

- Promote romance fiction and its sub-genres
- Increase awareness of the variety and quality of books, and their authors
- Provide a forum for readers to communicate, share and explore all things romance fiction

Follow them on Twitter: @ARRAinc

Find them on Facebook:
https://www.facebook.com/pages/Australian-Romance-Readers-Association/328481653871212

Visit the ARRA website:
www.australianromancereaders.com.au

Visit the ARRA blog:
https://australianromancereaders.wordpress.com/

TWC Press

TWC Press is a unique publishing co-operative consisting of published authors from all walks of life, working collaboratively toward their goal: to bring exceptional romance fiction direct to readers. Their motto is: 'For the readers'—and every project, every decision is made with that in mind.

Follow them on twitter: @TWCPress

Find them on Facebook:
https://www.facebook.com/twcpress

Visit the TWC Press website: www.twcpress.com

Visit the TWC Press blog: http://twcpress.wordpress.com/

Previous releases include:

Timeless Encounters

For lovers of historical and fantasy romance, each time-travelling novella is set within different eras, varying from sweet, to sexy, to suspenseful, but all with a central theme: the timeless search for the perfect love.

Moonlit Encounters

A diverse collection of short romantic fiction, from eight different authors, in different genres, for all readers.

Coming soon:

Captive Encounters, **March 2015**

Heat, heart and handcuffs—a steamy collection of sizzling romantic fiction.

Available at all good retail and e-tail stores.

Tribal Law reading guide

This reading group guide for *Tribal Law* includes an introduction from the author, some fun facts, discussion questions and a Q&A with author Shannon Curtis. The suggested questions are intended to help you and your group find new and interesting angles and topics to discuss. We hope this will enhance your conversation and improve your enjoyment of the book.

The story behind the story

Tribal Law is a story born from readers. On 4 July 2014, a number of readers and writers gathered at the Better Read Than Dead bookstore (as mentioned in the story!), and filled out questionnaires on what they would like to read in a romance. Questions ranged from what colour hair/eyes for hero/heroine, to character traits and quirks, and the preferred sub-genre and cover concepts, as well as secondary characters. The TWC Press team collated all these responses, and Shannon Curtis, using this information, plotted and wrote what is now *Tribal Law*.

The initial plan was to write a short story, but the information gathered showed that readers put a lot more consideration into how they would like a story to unfold, and when ARRA asked if it was possible to write a novel instead of a short story, TWC Press said yes—and Shannon Curtis got to work. From forgetful heroines with an in-built truth radar, and a sexy scarred hero who made teeth his life's work, to families at war—internally and externally—and a paranormal world to embrace it all, *Tribal Law* is the manifestation of a reading group's wish list.

Fun facts

The most requested occupation for a main or secondary character was dental-related. Why—because it doesn't seem to have been done before.

Author's response: Possibly for good reason!

The Better Read Than Dead bookstore does actually exist, and was the venue where the plot-storming activity occurred.

Mad E Pizza is also a real restaurant, where all hungry readers and authors adjourned for a bite to eat on the night. Limoncello shots were had by all.

The red hatchback was a special request from a reader.

One of the most requested quirks for characters was either an eidetic memory or forgetfulness.

The home of the Galen brothers is based on the Salvatore Mansion from The Vampire Diaries.

Discussion questions

1   Was the book what you were expecting? Why or why not?

2   What do you see as the central theme for this novel?

3   Do you think Ryder's issues with his family were resolved? Why or why not?

4   Do you think Vassiliki should take Vivianne's job offer? Why or why not?

5   What do you think of the character, Dave the tattoo artist? What purpose do you think he served for the novel?

6   Which character/s left you with more questions about them than answers?

7   Why do you think Melissa hates miscreants?

8   If this became a series, which characters do you think deserve their own story? How would their story unfold?

9   What do you think happens to Ryder and Vassiliki in the next chapter of their romance?

10 If you had the opportunity, what would YOU want to see in a book? What kind of hero? Heroine? Theme? Plot?

Interview with Shannon Curtis

Q **What made you take on the challenge of writing 'to order' for the readers?**

A   I thought it would be a fun thing to do, and I always enjoy finding new ways to connect with readers, but this one was also intended as a special thank you. Finding out what readers wanted to see in a story, then giving that story to them was a unique method of saying thank you— thank you for reading our stories and supporting us.

Q **Were there suggestions readers put forward that you thought 'No. No way can I include that'?**

A   Yes. There was one request for a hero with a fear of oral sex due to a traumatic experience involving teeth. Couldn't quite wrap my mind around that one.

Q **Were there some ideas you were expecting that readers didn't include?**

A   It was probably more the opposite, that readers came up with ideas *I* wasn't expecting, but I guess it was a little surprising that there were no requests for reunions or secret babies.:)

Q **Will you be writing Hunter's story?**

A   Hunter is such a fun character to write—he has the potential to be a bit of a villain, or at least a wicked hero, and I'd love to explore him more, so who knows, Hunter's story could be on the horizon. Or one for Matthias … or Vivianne … or Taylor … or maybe even Seraphina. Anything is possible!

www.ingramcontent.com/pod-product-compliance
Lightning Source LLC
Chambersburg PA
CBHW031332170626
46807CB00002B/660